Abner Post,
Oct, 18, 1857.

FROM DAWN TO DAYLIGHT;

OR,

The Simple Story of a Western Home.

BY A MINISTER'S WIFE.

NEW YORK:
DERBY & JACKSON, 119 NASSAU STREET.
1859.

W. H. Tinson, Stereotyper

Geo. Russell & Co., Printers.

PREFACE.

Some years since, I prepared the following sketch of the life of a dear friend, with whose history I had been familiar. At the time, my only object was to shorten some of the lonely hours of a tedious convalescence, and to gratify and amuse my children. Nothing could have been further from my thoughts, than trusting myself to the tender mercies of public opinion. But months after, a clergyman's wife, visiting in the family, chanced to read the manuscript, and felt that, if published, it might do good by leading laymen to perceive how easily, by kindness, considerateness and prompt payment, they could strengthen their Pastor's hands, or, on the contrary, paralyze all his efforts and energy, by negligence, thoughtlessness and selfishness.

"On that hint I spake." The main story, or rather narrative, is literally true. Names and dates have been changed for obvious reasons, and in some few instances, I have resorted to *fiction*, by giving that which a people *should do*, instead of what they *did or did not do.* Therefore, should these pages meet their eyes and a "still small voice" point them to the original, of some parts of this picture, that same voice will acquit both their old friends, and also the narrator, of any disposition to exaggerate, "or set down aught in malice."

CONTENTS

CHAPTER XVIII.

CHAPTER XIX.

FROM DAWN TO DAYLIGHT.

CHAPTER I.

MARY AND HER MOTHER.

THE room is bright and cheerful, marked by neatness and comfort, rather than luxury or elegance. At a window, looking southward, over a magnificent lawn, and broad green meadows, sits a middle-aged matron, with whose dark brown hair, scarcely yet touched with silver, and delicately tinted cheek and lip, time has dealt so kindly, that many a city belle, faded and worn by the dissipation of a life of pleasure, would give half the jewels which glitter on her form, to secure but a small portion of her gentle beauty.

Her sewing lies unnoticed in her lap, as her eye wanders fondly over the peaceful scene before her, and yet all its quiet loveliness has not power to dispel the lines of deep, and somewhat troubled thought from her brow.

Spring will in a few days yield to brighter summer. The noble trees, scattered over the grounds, whose broad branches give promise of grateful shelter from summer sun or shower, are already covered with the half developed leaves of delicate green, and tiny spots of white, among the cherry and pear trees, are peering, roguishly, out from their winter hiding-places—sure token that in a few days the "Hill Farm" will be spangled with blossoms, and redolent with perfumery of nature's own distilling. The meadow is sparkling with the yellow cowslip and dandelion, and "the hale young farmer goes whistling at his plough," on the hill-side beyond.

Surely, there can be nothing here to encourage sorrow or sadness.

Rising from her seat, as if her reverie had at length settled some uncertainty in her own mind, she turns with a sigh toward a young girl—evidently an invalid—who is seated near her, at the east window, in a large, old-fashioned easy chair. Very beautiful to that fond mother's eye, is the delicate being before her. She, too, is gazing upon a landscape, even more enchanting than that from which her mother has just turned.

The broad lake, transformed into a sea of liquid gold, by the morning sun—the mighty hills, flashing back a glory borrowed from the same source, and all the wealth of wood, and field, and meadow are before her: then why should so deep a shadow rest upon so young a face, or tear after tear fall unheeded? But the mother's watchful eye is anxiously trying to read her thoughts, and not well pleased with the result of her scrutiny, she steps softly to her daughter's side, and putting back the rich auburn curls which have fallen over her brow, said—

"Mary, my dear child, why so sad to-day? You are fast regaining health and strength; and your father says he shall endeavor to give you a ride this afternoon. The season is so favorable; everything looks bright and hopeful. Indeed, I cannot see my daughter's spirits drooping now, when her heart should be overflowing with gratitude, for the mercies of the past few weeks."

"Dear mother, I will try to overcome this despondency. I was looking back upon the past, and trembling for the future; but at the same time, I trust, not forgetful of the unmerited blessings of the present."

"Leave the future with God, my child, and try to let the past be 'as a dream when one awaketh;' at least, that part of it which must, necessarily, give you pain to remember. It can do you no good to recall it, and will, most assuredly, retard your recovery. For myself, I feel too joyous, too grateful, that you are spared to us, to countenance any indulgence in unprofitable reminiscences. It has given me much pain, to see you so little cheerful. Think of those around us, whose homes have been made utterly desolate by this terrible disease, while the Lord 'has not suffered His destroying angel to come into our house to smite us.' Though scattered, we are still an unbroken band. Oh! how kindly has our God dealt with us?"

"I do, indeed, bear this in grateful remembrance, and bless God with all my powers, who has so mercifully given my life to your prayers. And oh! how thankful am I, dear mother, that you are now relieved from watching and anxiety, and can begin to rest. It has been the hardest part of my illness, to see you so exhausted and distressed.

But"—— and again the eyes of the young girl filled with tears, and she hesitated.

"But what, my dear child? I must know what it is that troubles you, Mary."

"Oh, mother! I almost dread to get about again. If father would only love George; if he could be made to realize how little true happiness depends on wealth, or the position which riches are supposed to give! I shrink from the ride with him to-day; I tremble every time I see him alone, lest he should renew all the old sorrows, and insist upon my yielding to his wishes in regard to Mr. Dalton; and that, mother, I can never, never do."

"Be calm, my daughter, and listen. I have good news for you, which I supposed you were too weak to bear just yet. Had I thought of your very natural anxiety, however, I should not have delayed this information till now. You need fear no further annoyance, on this dreaded subject. You have nothing now to do but get well as fast as possible; and I, meanwhile, must school myself to feel ready to give you to George next fall. We learned last night that Dalton was married a week since to a lady in Boston. But, my poor child, you must be calm;" for Mary, while listening to her mother's words, had been greatly agitated, and now burst into uncontrollable weeping.

"Bear with me a few moments, dear mother. These foolish tears will do me no harm."

Mary, though young, had acquired self-control through many a sharp lesson, and was soon able to subdue the excitement which her mother's words had occasioned.

"Does father know of this?" she said, at length.

"Oh, yes. He heard the rumor some days since, but gave it no credence till last evening, when he met a friend of Mr. Dalton's at 'Spring's Store,' who was one of the attendants on the occasion; and, with the evident intention of irritating your father, most officiously narrated all the circumstances, in as public a manner as possible."

"Please tell me how father received it."

"I trust he had too much self-respect to manifest any annoyance, or receive it otherwise than with indifference, before so many listeners; but, you know, he had quite set his heart on this thing, though during your illness he seemed to drop the matter forever, and leave you to choose for yourself. Yet, of course, he was somewhat excited last night. I think, however, as much by the insulting way in which the intelligence was given, and the slight put upon you—as it was evidently intended he should consider it—as by any great disappointment in losing Dalton; for, from some things that have, accidentally, come to my knowledge, I fancy the purse-proud fellow, in his two last interviews, manifested an arrogance and disrespect which your father would not have tolerated, if again repeated. These last few weeks have, to be sure, enabled him to think more reasonably than he could do while constantly excited by that man. Yet, I greatly mistake if Dalton's overbearing temper had not in a short time so disgusted him, that you would have been left free, even if you had not been ill."

"Well, mother, this intelligence accounts for the sharp tone in which father spoke to me this morning. I feared a renewal of everything that has combined to make my life miserable the past year, and have been heart-sick ever since."

"But now, my child, thank God, who has 'turned your mourning into minstrelsy,' and ever try to bear in mind that your dear father's wish was to bring about that which he *thought would really* make you happy in the end; and if age and infirmity may have caused him to appear self-willed, and to judge incorrectly, you must forget it, and think of him ever with confidence and love.

"I shall leave you now, darling, to rest till dinner, that you may have strength and spirits for your afternoon ride."

"Never fear but I shall, dearest mother. It was the anxiety I have felt on this subject that has retarded my recovery, but now I feel as light-hearted and cheerful as a bird."

CHAPTER II.

HILL FARM.

WHILE the now happy Mary is resting from the excitement of the foregoing conversation, we will improve the opportunity to give such explanation as may be needed to interpret the introductory chapter, and also to make our readers acquainted with the worthy inmates of "Hill Farm."

Dr. John Leighton was the youngest son of a kind, hard working, but quite uneducated farmer, in one of the smallest and most obscure towns in good old Massachusetts. He was among the first settlers of the place, and as his family rapidly multiplied around him, it was no easy task to make his large, but sterile farm meet all their necessities, and yet keep free from debt—DEBT! No ghost or goblin, conjured up in olden times by designing priests, to frighten poor ignorant mortals into abject compliance with their wickedness, ever held more powerful dominion over any human being, than that word possessed over Moses Leighton. Brave, as simple hearted, it was all on earth that he feared. It conveyed to his mind the only distinct idea of what "*the* unpardonable sin" must mean; at any rate, it was so great a wrong "that he would never have forgiven *himself* if guilty of it." No labor was too hard, no deprivation worth a thought, so long as he could with honest pride, lay his hand upon his heart and say, "I owe no man a penny." When, therefore, John expressed a wish to prepare for the practice of medicine, his father was utterly confounded. Where was the money to come from? "Farming, shoemaking, and black smith work, had done well enough for himself and his elder boys—preaching was all right, if any one had a 'gift' that way—but *lawyers* were always meddling with other people's quarrels, and he really must think that *doctors* put more into the grave-yard, than they ever kept out. Why couldn't Johnny be contented to do like the rest of the family, and not wish to set himself above them?"

At length, after many discussions, it was settled in family council, that "arter all, Johnny never did love to work, and doctoring, was, may be, 'bout all he'd ever be good for."

And thereupon John Leighton left home, and struggled through difficulties and trials that would have disheartened any but a sturdy son of New England, until he had secured a sufficient education for the profession he had chosen.

A year's trial convinced the staid people of the little village where he at first established himself, and who, it must be confessed, had been rather displeased with the tall, pale young doctor's somewhat foppish air, that he had, as they expressed it, "something to him."

In seven years he stood higher in his profession than any of the neighboring physicians, and began to feel that the place was too strait for him.

In the early part of his public life he had married a woman several years younger than himself, of a most lovely disposition, and exalted character. Her whole life was devoted to the service of her husband and children, and every opportunity which enabled her to aid in carrying out his plans, was a great addition to her happiness. When, therefore, he one day informed her of an unexpected opening for his business, in a large and flourishing town near by, and that at the same time he had been urged to buy the well known

Hill Farm, in that place, he found her, as usual, ready to coöperate, yet fully aware of the additional labor and responsibility which must, of necessity, come upon herself. There was but one point that inclined them to hesitate at all. Both had been educated to feel the greatest reluctance to take any step that might involve them in pecuniary obligations.

If Dr. Leighton made the contemplated change, he would be obliged, at once, to assume a debt of several thousands, and, as in those primitive days, a fortune was not made in a day—nor lost as rapidly—it would be a work of time, and the most rigid economy to free themselves from the burden, and rejoice once more in true independence. With courageous hearts, however, they calmly judged themselves, and both felt that they were capable of making the effort—a blooming daughter and three fine sons, being, in their estimation, incentives sufficient for any exertion.

They argued wisely, that a farm was the best place to give strength and health to their sons, and establish in them such habits of industry and perseverance, as were most likely to insure their becoming men of the right stamp, whatever vocation they might choose, when old enough to judge for themselves, and that the same habits would secure true worth to their beloved daughter.

The change was made. Hill Farm became the happy home of Dr. Leighton and his family. Twenty years passed swiftly by. Ten "brave lads and merry lassies" had made the old halls vocal with their glee. Of course it could not be expected that so long a period would bring only unmixed happiness; for Hill Farm was of the earth. The "trail of the serpent" was visible even here. In the loved circle, sin, and consequently sorrow, had often sought and found a temporary shelter; and many a hard battle had been fought, before the foe, once received, could be expelled. Yet in all these years, Death's dark shadow had never fallen on their home; and though their loved ones were beginning to disperse, in various ways, they could still feel that theirs was an unbroken family.

Four of the children, happy, and highly respected, were settled near the old homestead.

Three sons, having by patient economy toiled through a college education, had entered the ministry, and now stood before the world noble-hearted, zealous champions for the truth. Mary and her two youngest brothers were all that remained with their parents.

The farm was paid for. It had been no light task to bring forward so large a family, and yet cancel all liabilities; but it had been bravely met; father, mother, sons and daughters, each in their sphere, lending a helping hand, and cheerfully and lovingly, bearing one another's burdens. The daughters were energetic and capable, the sons ready to meet life's changes with cheerful self-reliance and Christian courage, and the character of the judicious mother, sincerely loved by friends and neighbors, and well-nigh idolized by her family, shone all the brighter for every trial.

But it would have been marvellous had all come from the contest unscathed. Unfortunately, Dr. Leighton, in this long and severe struggle for independence and competence, had learned to place too high an estimate on wealth; and, just when freed from pecuniary embarrassments, his wife and children began to feel that they might take life a little easier, and enjoy the fruits of their mutual industry; he became even more close and calculating, and what, in past days, had been only necessary economy, was now, in old age, fast tending toward a morbid penuriousness.

He was by nature, though passionate and somewhat exacting, a large-hearted and affectionate man. Mrs. Leighton's gentle firmness and quiet management had warded off many a storm, which, but for her, would have shipwrecked some of her children, and perhaps destroyed the happiness of others. As age and over-exertion began to affect the doctor's powerful frame and excellent constitution, his temper was less under control, and this, joined to his increasing love of wealth, threatened to darken the life of his noble partner and the younger children.

A year before our history commences, Mary became acquainted, through one of her brothers, with a young gentleman of great worth and superior talents. Thrown often into each other's society, as was but natural, the acquaintance soon ripened into strong attachment; and when George Herbert, with manly frankness, made known his wishes to her parents, Mrs. Leighton gave a cordial approval, and the doctor had too great a respect for talent and intellectual superiority, to withhold his consent, though, truth to tell, it was not given as cheerfully as could have been wished. If the engagement might have been consummated in the course of a few months, he would have felt no hesitation. There was no other claimant for his daughter's hand at the time, and George, by his respectful attention, had secured a strong hold on Dr. Leighton's affections. But the young man had consecrated himself to the work of the ministry, and some years must elapse before he could feel prepared to enter upon the labors of that profession. Both Mary and himself were young—too young to think of immediate marriage, even had he been all prepared, and they had too much confidence in each other's truth, to apprehend any danger from a protracted engagement.

The old gentleman, however, saw "lions in the way" on every side.

Something disastrous was sure to happen. "Long engagements never did turn out well," and this would only be the repetition of the old story: a false lover and broken-hearted damsel, long before Herbert's education was completed.

But the only lion that could alarm Mrs. Leighton or her daughter, intruded all too soon under the guise of a large fortune, encumbered with a self-conceited young man, utterly devoid of delicacy, and nothing doubting but that half a million could buy the fairest lady in the land. The slight obstacle of a prior engagement—what was that, before such a pile of gold?

Mrs. Leighton and the brothers and sisters left no honorable means untried to conceal the knowledge of Mr. Dalton's wishes from Mary's father, too well aware that the prospect of an immediate settlement and unlimited wealth would have a power over his mind, which once he would have scorned to recognize.

The eldest brother was the first to whom the man of dollars condescended to declare his intention to honor Miss Mary with his name and fortune; but he was frankly told that her heart was no longer in her own keeping. With the simplicity of an honest mind, Robert Leighton supposed a gentleman would need nothing more, to show the impropriety of any further advances. Judge of his indignation when the purse-proud man, in the most patronizing manner, begged leave to assure Mr. Leighton that such a trifle would never cause him the least uneasiness. He was proud to have it in his power to place Miss Mary in so enviable a position, that she could not fail to forget all that girlish romance, and her friends might rest satisfied that she would never be reminded by him of this amiable weakness. Whereupon he was emphatically assured that the young lady, as well as her friends, was perfectly satisfied with her youthful choice, and could never experience the slightest drawings toward Mr. Dalton, or his omnipotent money-bags.

He left young Leighton determined on making a personal application to Mary, confident that his charms must prove irresistible. "Just as though," said he to a crony, "Miss Leighton will dream of refusing a position of ease and affluence, together with a clever young fellow, like myself, for limited means and a poor parson! No, no. The Leightons won't forget so readily how much toil and self-denial they encountered to secure their present position. Trust me, she will not say me nay."

Warned by her brother of Dalton's determination, Mary carefully avoided all society where she would be in danger of meeting him; but the fear that he might make application to her father, was a source of great anxiety to herself and mother;

for unspoken in the heart of both, was the foreboding of great sorrow, should he learn that Mary had refused so dazzling an offer.

In a short time he succeeded in forcing himself into her presence, and was politely but most decidedly refused, and on leaving the room, coolly assured her he should not consider her answer as final until he had seen Dr. Leighton himself. This threat was soon acted upon, and of course, the old gentleman resolved that if Mary did not know what was for her own good, she must be compelled to understand it.

From that dark day, poor Mrs. Leighton and her daughter were equally persecuted.

Dalton besieged the house; and when refused an interview, the doctor's anger was violently aroused. Many months went by, and happiness seemed forever banished from that once peaceful habitation. George Herbert was far away, and delicacy would not permit his being informed of the trials to which his poor Mary was subjected.

To the heart-sick girl, earth was fast becoming a dreary place. Her father, who had in happier days been more indulgent to her, as the youngest daughter, than any of his flock, now seldom spoke, except in anger, or to insist upon her listening to Dalton's addresses.

But there was a sad rebuke in store for his misguided heart. That dreaded scourge, the scarlet fever, had been very severe during the winter and spring. Dr. Leighton was in constant requisition, his reputation for skill and sound judgment, in acute disease, being still unimpaired. The fatigue of day and night service, at his advanced age, of course had a tendency to make him more than usually irritable when at home.

One evening he entered his house under great excitement. Dalton had, it appeared, been urging strong measures—assuring the doctor that he would give up the pursuit, if Mary could not be brought to *obey her father;* and smarting under the imputation of inability to control his household, he forgot himself, and words were spoken, which, before morning, he would have given worlds to recall.

Mary had been drooping for some days, and before the sun again brightened her pleasant chamber with his morning rays, she was smitten by the fearful disease which had made such sad havoc in many a neighbor's home.

Oh, how her father's heart reproached him, when, in the delirium of fever, she entreated him to love poor Mary again, and not break her heart; and then again wildly calling upon George to shield her from such harsh treatment, and take her away.

Suns waxed and waned—hope died out from the mother's heart, and none may tell that father's anguish, when, turning from her bedside, on the fourteenth morning, in reply to his poor wife's earnest look, he said:

"My dear! There is no hope! I have done all I can!" and the strong man bowed his head on her shoulder and wept like a child.

"Oh! my bird! my pet, my darling Mary! If she would but rally long enough to forgive her hard old father! Confound that Dalton! It is enough to drive me mad, to think that I should have been willing to yield my own sweet dove to such a fool for the sake of his dollars!"

"Hush, dear husband," said Mrs. Leighton. "Look at our child!"

Her eyes were turned full on her father's face, and for the first time in many days, beamed with intelligence. A bright smile flashed across her wan cheek, speaking as plainly as words could have done, of love and forgiveness for him, and peace and comfort for herself. A moment it lingered, and then the fever burned more fiercely than before.

For hours those sorrowing parents, and her weeping brothers and sisters, hung over her, fearing each breath would be the last. At length she slept, and anxious watchers hushed their own heart-throbs, to listen to her breathings. Time passed unheeded by that mournful group. Breakfast and dinner had been served, but none moved from the side of the pale sleeper. Darkness once more brooded over the Hill Farm when Mary woke —the fearful disease had spent its force, and she was saved.

Four weeks had elapsed since that eventful evening, and Mary, though convalescing, was not yet strong. An irritable word from her father had awakened all her old fears.

The doctor had heard of Dalton's marriage the previous evening, while attending to some business at the village store. A large number of idlers were lounging around, and the manner in which the intelligence was communicated was exceedingly vexatious, and this, together with the thought that the wealth which might have been his daughter's, was now lost to her, had irritated him exceedingly. But his really good sense, and kind heart, soon banished all regrets, and he was able to recall the memory of his own youthful days, and to feel that wealth was not necessary to his child's peace or happiness. He saw that he had distressed her greatly by his petulance in the morning, and during their ride exerted himself to dispel every shade of uneasiness from her mind. The ride was delightful, and Mary returned refreshed and comforted.

"And now, dear mother," said she, when she had told Mrs. Leighton how pleasantly the time had passed, "I begin to feel well and strong already. The certainty that I have nothing more to fear from Dalton has removed a burden from my mind which kept me constantly anxious; but you need feel no further anxiety on my account. I consider myself no longer on the sick list."

CHAPTER III.

LEAVING HOME.

Two weeks after the incidents recorded in the last chapter, we again find Mrs. Leighton and her daughter seated in Mary's pleasant chamber.

They are speaking of the changes which a few months will, probably, make in their circumstances.

"It makes me sad, mother, when I think how lonely you and father will soon be. Are you aware that both Henry and John have no taste for a farmer's life, and are only waiting for some opening, by which they can make the attempt to secure a collegiate education?"

A shadow, for a moment, crossed Mrs. Leighton's face; but all traces of feeling were instantly suppressed, and she replied, calmly:

"I ought not to be surprised, though I can hardly realize that your brothers have passed out from boyhood and should soon be prepared to take their places among men. It is the lot of all parents to bring their loved ones on, step by step, till a mother's care and a father's control are no longer necessary, and then, like the young birds you were watching so intently yesterday, we must be willing to see them spread their wings, and seek a nest of their own."

"It was of *that* I was thinking; and how our mother, like that gentle bird, forgetting her own sorrow, encourages and strengthens us for our flight."

"That is not so very hard to do, my dear, when the mother sees all her children seeking the right path, and ready to labor for the best good of mankind, especially when sure, as I am, that however distant, my children's hearts will ever turn lovingly to the dear old homestead, and to the parents sheltered there."

"Well, now!" cried Johnny, bursting gaily into the room, "if here isn't our lady mother and demure sister Mary, looking for all the world as if they were just entering a convent! Halloo! Harry, come here. Wouldn't Mrs. Dr. Leighton make a grand Lady Abbess? Wonder what father would say to that? Doesn't she look as though she had just finished a lecture to sis, on the beauty and happiness of single blessedness? Say, Mayflower, doesn't mother wish you to take the *white veil?* If so, the document Harry was bringing you may as well go into the fire."

"Not so at all, Johnny," said Harry. "I'm much mistaken if it has not more to do toward procuring a *white veil* than all our bonnie mother's lectures. I wouldn't wonder if it's a homily from a certain devout priest, who is willing to take the troublesome office of confessor to Lady Mary Leighton. You may be sure he'll urge the importance of taking *certain vows* as soon as may be. But, say, sister mine, shall I burn this, as yonder scapegrace advises?" And the laughing Harry held up the letter.

A glance at Mary's blushing face would have revealed the writer, if the post-mark had not done so before.

"Long looked for, come at last. If master George doesn't give a satisfactory reason for making you wait so long, I shall challenge him to meet Harry and myself in the 'Long Lot,' with scythes for weapons, and we'll soon teach the young parson a lesson."

"Leave your sister in peace, young giddy pates," said Mrs. Leighton, "and come with me."

"But, mother, I feel it my duty (and painful though it be, I shall follow the path of duty *straight out*, as good Deacon Tombs says) to inform our young novice here, that I have heard of a widow, 'with a right smart chance' of money, out in those western wilds, who has been impressed with the belief that she is destined to take charge of George herself. Can he resist her golden charms, Mary, as faithfully as you did a certain"——

"Now, Johnny, you carry your jesting too far, and asserting my rights, I shall command you to leave my domains," said his sister, rising. Her brother caught her in his arms and showered a score of kisses on hands, face and brow, in revenge, as he said, for being so rudely dismissed, and then, with his mother and brother, left the room.

The letter evidently agitates our fair friend, and, availing ourselves of an author's invisibility and privilege, we will purloin the contents, and soon learn what has so suddenly driven the roses from her cheek.

GLENVILLE, *June* 9, 1—.

MY DEAREST MARY:

I have delayed writing the past two weeks, even at the risk of giving you some anxious hours, that I might decide upon a proposition of great importance to us both. It required much careful deliberation, and, as I could not be with you to talk it over, and must give an answer before letters could pass between us, I preferred, for your peace of mind, dear one, to say nothing till I could give you some definite information.

I have received and accepted a call to become pastor of the church in this place. I preached my first regular sermon here the first of May, and have supplied the pulpit for the three last Sabbaths.

The place is small, and many of my friends think I ought to secure a larger field. But I shall find more than I can do to my own satisfaction, I doubt not, and much prefer a young church to one that has become wedded to certain notions, which they will consider it sacrilege to gainsay or resist.

And now, my own Mary, does not your heart interpret my wishes? Is it not desirable that we should begin life's real work together?

I am to be ordained in six weeks or two months. I want my *wife* with me on that interesting occasion, and I feel that I cannot be denied. I cannot think as I ought of anything else, till I receive your answer.

May I come for you one month from to-day; and will you be ready to leave, with me, for *our home* the week after?

Dear Mary, the home I offer has little to attract, unless the love, which has so long been yours, can adorn and beautify. I sometimes feel that it is selfish to remove you from all the comforts which surround you, to the toil and hardship which must inevitably fall to your lot, if you give yourself to me. But *that* you have already done—have you not? and I have no magnanimous intention of offering to resign you to that knight of the Golden Fleece, that Harry has warned me of. Ah, Mary! It is high time I had you safe under my own care!

Dearest, I know you were sincere when you promised your love to me, and for all these years you have not swerved, under many temptations (God bless you)! and now, you will not hesitate to grant my request, even though it be a few months earlier than we at first anticipated? I shall be restless and troubled till I hear from you. Do not delay. I can write no more now, and yet I feel that I have said nothing as I could wish.

Ever yours, my own dear girl,

GEORGE HERBERT.

Mary had been accustomed to seek her mother when she had read her western letters—for Mrs. Leighton was her children's confidant in all things—but now, after waiting a long time, she sought her daughter's chamber, hardly knowing why she felt uneasy. Mary sat holding her open letter in her hand, but so deep in thought, that she did not observe her mother, till she stood by her side, and anxiously inquiring if she had received anything to distress her. "Nothing to distress, dear mother; but much to sober me." And she at once read the letter.

Both sat silent for many minutes, and when Mrs. Leighton at last spoke, her voice had lost something of its accustomed calmness.

"We have looked forward to this so long, my child—that I, for one, thought I was prepared to meet it more courageously; yet, now it comes over me like a new thought. How can I learn to do without you, my darling! But this is foolish, I should set you an example of courage?

"Lay by your letter for the present, and come with me into the garden. We shall both think more cheerfully in the fresh, pure air, than in your chamber. We have many days, yet, in which to accustom ourselves to the change proposed."

"But, mother, I must answer this letter immediately; and what can I—what ought I to say to George?"

"Your answer cannot go before the morning's mail, and you must come with me now. You are pale and weary with anxious thought. The evening will be soon enough for your letter."

The mother and daughter passed at once from the chamber to the garden, and after lingering awhile among its pleasant walks, and watching the sun go down through gorgeous clouds, they returned to the house—Mary to write the important letter, and Mrs. Leighton to break the matter to her husband and sons.

We will not dwell upon the history of the next few weeks. The joys and sorrows, hopes and fears, belonging to those last days, when a young, warm-hearted girl prepares to leave father and mother, brother and sister, to go forth with the chosen one, need no description.

The old have not forgotten—the young will soon understand it by experience.

The last words are spoken—the last fond kisses exchanged, and tearful, but full of love and hope, the young bride passes from the home of her childhood. What changes ere she may enter it again! Does he who now gazes fondly on the fair being by his side, realize all the responsibility he has so gladly assumed? Will he deal gently with her always—remembering that he is now her all—that for his dear sake, she leaves every tie, and each familiar scene, to follow him into a land of strangers, and that whatever of care and labor may be in store for him, *she* has a *claim* on his time and thoughts, stronger than any other? Will he never forget this claim—or, as years roll by, will not contact with the conflicting elements of this busy world, so wean his thoughts from the wife of his youth that a wish expressed by her for a share of his society, or at least a *small portion* of his hours of relaxation, may appear to him exacting or unkind?

Ah, this unintentional selfishness, so common to literary and public men, has caused more domestic unhappiness than aught else save intemperance. They have so many things to perplex and harass them—they are wearied with anxious thought for the good of their people, or by close research and investigation upon literary subjects, and the mind must rest, or change entirely the current of thought. They do not, by any means, intend to neglect their home treasures, and are not conscious that they do. But new acquaintances are gradually formed—a word must be given to this one, a few moments to that, or just a step to glance at this curiosity till all the leisure time has flown, and the public servant must return to duties which require his undivided attention, and, perhaps, not one word or look has been saved for home. If, after many such experiences, the wife ventures a timid remonstrance, a sharp rebuke may be the reply; no doubt, repented as soon as uttered, but the conscience is easily silenced, by "Well, I did not mean to speak so impatiently; but she is unreasonable. She should not forget that a public man has duties, in the way of trifling attentions to those interested in him, and—and—well, I'll be more careful in future." But conscience, thus silenced, does not long ward off other, and more severe rebuffs, and it takes but a few years of such teaching, to make a wife *fear* as well as *love;* and, if sometimes wearied with longing for a few loving words, sick, and overburdened with many cares, her sense of right and justice overcome both fear and love, and she speaks plain *truths*—such as a *wife* can never, *safely*, venture upon—most likely she increases the evil instead of remedying it. Oh! *why* need this *ever* be so, when deep in the heart of both, burns a love stronger than death?

But, thanks be to God, there are many glorious exceptions, and that, too, among the most prominent of public and literary men. There are those whose hearts are springs, which no labor or adverse circumstances can quench; whom God has so abundantly endowed, that, while the home garden, as the source and centre, is always fresh and decked with unfading flowers, the overflow of this glad, living-stream, freshens and brightens, and purifies the whole region around, sending love, kindness, and unfailing cheerfulness wherever it flows. Blessed among women is the wife of such a one! It matters not how unpropitious may be all else that can surround her, the consciousness of so safe a resting-place will lighten toil, and bring pleasure out of pain.

CHAPTER IV.

THE BRIDAL TRIP.

We left our young friends, rather unceremoniously, at the beginning of their bridal tour, to make some grave reflections, which they, at least, will deem entirely uncalled for.

A letter or two, from Mary to her mother, will give the particulars of her journey.

"Pittsburg, *Sept.* —, 18—.

"Dear Mother:

"You doubtless received my short note from New York; and I now employ my first leisure moment, in this city of coal and smoke, to give you the history of our journey thus far.

"We went by railroad across New York State; my first experience with the '*iron horse*' you know. I had felt somewhat timid when I thought of trying this, to me, unusual mode of travelling. Johnny will remember some lines purporting to be the defiance of this fiery Bucephalus:

"'Fetter me strong with your iron bands,
Be sure of your curb and rein;
For I scorn the might of your puny hands,
As the tempest laughs at chains.'

"Well, after thus throwing the gauntlet in the face of all travellers, my impression was, that I shouldn't feel at all 'sure of the curb and rein.' I didn't wish George to suspect me of such folly, for I imagine he would be a good deal mortified, if his wife supposed herself at liberty to start, and scream, and show off many of those little fancy airs, which wiser brides than I pretend to be, are sometimes accustomed to consider a part of the honeymoon privileges.

"Having guessed this much of my spouse's character, you must know I had for many days been laying up a large stock of fortitude and courage for this very journey.

"But isn't it too provoking, dear mother, to have made all this preparation for nothing? Perhaps I may thank my noisy, frolicksome brothers for a large share of my self-possession; for I really doubt if the huge black nondescript, that flew with us, over the road, is capable of making more unearthly sounds than I have often heard in and about my own loved home. At any rate, I flatter myself, George never once thought I was a novice in railroad travelling.

"I did, indeed, wince a little, when I first heard the hideous shriek of the steam-whistle, and again, when composedly reading, in broad daylight, I found myself, of a sudden, in Egyptian darkness, I involuntarily caught hold of George's arm. To be sure, I recovered instantly, and meant to have passed it off as a *love token*, but the ingrate gravely remarked: 'Don't be alarmed, Mary, we are only passing through the tunnel.' 'So I perceive,' I demurely replied; and as we began to catch glimpses of sunlight, I slily glanced into his face, to see if my ruse was successful. Imagine my vexation, when I saw that curl of the lip, and roguish twinkle of the eye which I have so often enjoyed when *others* were the occasion of it. I think after this, I will make no pretensions to more than I am capable of sustaining; certainly not for some time, at least.

"My husband, however, has to-day been manœuvering to pass himself off in my eyes as a deep thinker—an exceedingly absent-minded man—and, in truth, he so nearly succeeded that I shouldn't like him to repeat the experiment.

"We changed cars at the station, where we dined. During these changes, everything, to the uninitiated, is perfect confusion; and, as trains are passing in all directions, there is danger that the verdant traveller should make a mistake, and, crab-like, go backward.

"George, therefore, charged me to remain *just in that place.* No matter what running to and fro I might see, I was not to stir from that window till he had looked after the baggage, when he would be sure and come for me in season. I obeyed his direction, literally, like a dutiful wife.

"After a short time, from the window where I stood, I saw a gentleman take a seat in a train that seemed all ready to start, and deliberately commence reading a paper. Surely that is George! Why didn't he come for me? Yes, it is! No mistake about that. Well, I needn't worry. He told me on no account to leave this window, till he called me. But there is the bell! Gentlemen are calling for their wives, mothers hurrying across the platform with their children, and he remains immovable. If I should be left! I can endure it no longer. I hastened to the door: 'George!' I couldn't forbear smiling, even then, at his look of utter dismay. The cars began to move. With one bound he gained the platform, and, aided by the conductor, succeeded in *swinging* me on board!

"We both sat *very still* for some minutes; I shan't tell you in what words he apologized, but if he ever laughs at me about my unlucky *affectionateness*, when passing through *that tunnel*, I shall, assuredly, remind him of his attempted desertion of the wife of a week.

"*He* says it was *absent-mindedness.* But how do I know that he did not intend leaving me there, in the wilderness, without money, clothes, or friends? At any rate, I mean to lay it up as a weapon of defence. May I not, mother?

"Soon after we had finished talking over this little incident, the conductor came to examine our tickets. But an instant before, George had left my side. 'Ticket, madam!' I looked for my husband, but not seeing him, replied, 'The gentleman with me has it."

"'What name?' 'Miss Leighton.' He looked carefully through the list of passengers on his book. 'I don't see any such name—did I understand aright?' 'Miss Leighton, sir.' 'Ah, yes, Leighton—well, let me see,' and again his eye ran over the names. It was becoming very annoying, for the attention of the passengers was drawn toward us. 'I can't find it;' and this time there was a touch of incredulity in his tone. 'Will you please see if *you* can find the name yourself, madam!'

"Of course I took the book in the most confident manner, and I dare say, with a look of injured innocence. Up and down all those lines my eye wandered, but no 'Miss Leighton' was there. The letters ran together—the names began a wild fantastic dance over the pages—I saw a storm gathering in the conductor's eye—I raised my head to meet the worst, and there stood that most inveterate of all teases, suffocating with merriment. He came forward at this crisis, and taking a seat by my side, said, 'If you will look for *Mrs. Herbert* instead of *Miss* Leighton, you will find it all right. The lady is not quite familiar with her own name!'

"This is a specimen of the life I am to expect, I presume. Well, my dear brothers have given me some lessons beforehand.

"I must close this long letter, I have wearied you all, I fear. I kept on writing, with little of interest to tell, just because it seemed so like talking with you all once more.

"Good night, and blessings on you all, my own loved ones. George unites in love.

"You shall hear again as soon as we reach the end of our journey.

"Ever yours, lovingly,

"MARY HERBERT."

"GLENVILLE, *Sept.* —, 18—.

"MY DEAREST MOTHER:

"You will see by the post-mark that we are *home* at last. How strange to speak of any spot, but Hill Farm, as home!

"I have little of interest to tell connected with our journey from Pittsburg to this place, or rather, that which was exceedingly interesting to me, I might not be able to make so to you. I have, to tell the truth, been a little ashamed of my last epistle, and imagine I hear father say, 'Pshaw! does the silly girl suppose that these little honeymoon adventures will have the same charm to the 'old folks at home,' 'that they have to her.' Excuse it, this once, dear father. I'm the *minister's wife* now, and you'll see how grave

I shall be; at least I hope you will. I haven't become so accustomed to my honors as to feel quite sure that I shall wear them with proper dignity.

"We arrived at this place about noon, and were met by one of George's elders, Mr. Blake, with whom we are to board for the present. I was so well prepared by my husband's descriptions, that I was not greatly surprised, when we picked our way from the wharf to the house *through mud and over pigs;* but my first impression was, that we should find these *two* articles, the staple commodity of this far-famed region.

"The village is on the banks of the river, and certainly can boast of but little beauty, though I ought not to judge till I have seen more.

"Most of the houses are low, brown cottages—many ranking no higher than log-cabins. Our host's dwelling is a pretty, two-story white house, with a fine veranda in front, but built too near the road, and with but a few shade-trees. He is a man of wealth, and abundantly able to live in more fashionable style.

"But he has married a frugal Yankee girl (he is himself of Dutch decent), and both agree, I presume, in preferring comfort to gentility. There I agree with them, though I can't quite understand why her eastern education has not made her feel the *necessity* of a few more *conveniencies.* But that is not my business. I ought rather to be learning how to do without many things, which I have been accustomed to consider indispensable.

"Should we ever attempt to keep house, it will be on a very small pattern. That gives me no uneasiness however. I flatter myself, I could find considerable amusement in contriving to do with as little as possible.

"Last night was my first real experience of the torments which the mosquito is capable of inflicting. You know brother Robert used to tell long yarns about them; but I always suspected him of a slight exaggeration. I beg his pardon, most humbly, now. I am well paid for the injustice I did him, however; verily, the half was not told me. If you could only see me! Face, neck, and arms are speckled and swollen out of all resemblance to my former self. And to-day I am to receive calls from our parishioners! They will not accuse their pastor of marrying for beauty, that's certain; but of course they will presume it must have been *goodness* which captivated him. Alas! for the time when they discover their mistake!

"And here they come. Oh! how I dread these first introductions.

"*Evening.*—The day is over at last, and I am at liberty to converse a while with the dear home circle.

"I judge we must have received calls from nearly all who will come under my husband's care. And such a variety, I would not have believed to belong to one country.

"The most grotesque styles of dress; the funniest and most uncouth mode of expression! But I will not allow myself to criticise these trifling peculiarities. They are '*our people*,' with whom we are to be associated for years—may be for life—in whose well-being we must feel the deepest interest.

"I shall soon become accustomed to all that now strikes me as singular. I hope to make them love me, and am sure it will be no hard matter to love them in return.

"There was one old lady, in whom I am already

greatly interested. She reminds me, dear mother, so much of *your* father, in person; and I much mistake if she has not many of his mental excellences, only she lacks the cheerful, joyous look he always wore. I am confident she has a history worth hearing. Her face is very pleasant to look upon; but there is a subdued and saddened expression about her, that speaks plainly of suffering, or heart-trials. She is very kind and lady-like in her manner, and I already feel more drawn toward her than any one I have seen since I left you.

"Another quiet, gentle lady, with three pretty daughters, pleased me greatly. Her husband is a Methodist class-leader, but taught by his wife, I presume, he is very liberal in his feelings toward other denominations. I'm sure I shall love Mrs. Gilbert. But I was sorry to see indications of very feeble health. Indeed, no one thing has struck me so unpleasantly, as the pale, sallow, unhealthy-looking people I have met, so far, since I came here. I have not seen one clear, rosy-cheeked person, such as we meet constantly in New England; and yesterday, before my face was so disfigured by the ravages of the mosquitoes, I was asked several times if I had not a 'fever spell' upon me, because my cheeks were so red!

"Among those presented, were several who will teach me caution, I imagine. At any rate, I felt that they came to 'spy out the land,' and make reports. But such persons are common everywhere; and I presume, on further acquaintance, I shall find many lovable qualities, even in them.

"Just before tea, I walked with George and Mr. Blake as far as *our church*. It is a small, unpainted building, capable of seating about as many as the 'school-house' near the church at home. It certainly has no architectural beauties, externally, or adornments, internally, to distract attention from the word spoken; but, nevertheless, it may be quite as likely to prove the 'very gate of heaven,' as many of our splendid eastern churches.

"I must close, from fatigue, for, aside from unpacking trunks and 'putting things to rights' in our little room, and receiving many calls, I have been very busy making a *net*, to protect us from our enemies to-night. It is a common arrangement here, but I am quite dubious about it. I fancy I shall prefer, out of two evils, feasting the little savages, to being smothered. It makes me gasp for breath, even now, to think of becoming a prisoner under this curious affair.

"Good night. George unites in warmest love.

"Most affectionately,

"Mary Herbert."

CHAPTER V.

PREPARING A HOME.

MR. and Mrs. Herbert have now fairly entered upon their labors. There was much in their situation to perplex and dishearten, but they came prepared for it all, and found their courage rising as difficulties met them.

The church was but a handful, composed chiefly of the poor and illiterate. The wealthy, and more intellectual class of the population were attendants on the Methodist church, that being the fashionable denomination. This little church had almost died out; and when Mr. Herbert was first requested to supply the pulpit, neither he, nor those who invited him, had a thought of its being but for the one Sabbath. But he was full of life and freshness, and possessed of a mind of no common order. His manner of preaching was something original. It *woke* them up. They were not quite prepared to decide whether it *was best* to be so thoroughly aroused. It was not exactly comfortable; but at any rate there could be no great harm in trying it once more. The next Sabbath the little building was crowded, and many, from other churches, were present.

There was no longer a doubt. The satisfaction was general; and all, even other sects, felt that a man like the new preacher would be a public blessing. But could he be induced to settle over so insignificant a church? They would give him a "call," at all events. The invitation was extended to him; and, although his friends were anxious he should look higher, yet his own judgment told him, in such a community, a large work could be done, and certainly few places needed it more.

Beside, the unusual interest manifested by all classes would seem an indication of Providence, that this was to be at least his first field of labor. And thus the matter was settled, and he has come, with his young bride, to cast in his lot among them.

Their church could only offer a very small compensation, and it was so inadequate to their necessities, that it was deemed advisable to board for the

3*

present, and even then, it would be difficult to tell how they were to get safely through the year.

But Mrs. Herbert was sanguine. There were many ways, she was quite sure, by which she could help eke out their scanty means. She had no false pride about laboring with her own hands. Her early training, at Hill Farm, had prepared her physically, for just the position she now held; and most heartily, as every day's experience disclosed some additional necessity for energy and industry, did she bless her mother for the ability, which she felt confident of possessing, to meet the emergencies before her.

Let me pause here one moment, to offer a few words for the serious consideration of those who have a Home Missionary's life in prospect.

I have known and seen much of the sufferings and trials, which await the wives of those who go out to our new States to preach the gospel. Let any one, who contemplates such a life, be sure that his chosen companion has health and strength for the task, and, withal, a *domestic education*, fitting her for the *labor, which cannot be avoided.* If she has not all these, the attempt to occupy such a field is throwing life and usefulness away.

None can tell, but those who have been tried, how soon the strongest constitutions droop before the difficulties and hard labor incident to limited means, in the generally unhealthy climate of our new States. I could point to many, many graves where rest true-hearted wives, who came, willing and anxious to aid their husbands in spreading the Gospel, but whose strength failed before the first few years of hardship and disease.

A more correct public sentiment is rapidly spreading over the whole country, but at the time of which I write, a clergyman's support was considered as *charity* in western life, and the small, very small amount *promised*, was not always paid. That "the *laborer* was worthy of his hire," none pretended to deny, but a *parson* wasn't one of those meant by that passage. "What labor can there be in dashing off two sermons on Sunday, and making an 'off hand' speech two or three times during the week days. And surely it is no hardship to run round and sit a while with the sick. A wedding and a funeral now and then can't be any great labor. Why, for my part, I think the preachers have a real easy time of it. And then the parson's *wife*, I can't see *why she* shouldn't milk the cows, and split the kindling-wood occasionally, and do the housework as well as my Betsey." Ah, yes! if that were all! But who remembers that added to all that "Betsey" does, the minister's wife must be out among the people, or they will find fault. She must head the Sewing Society and Maternal Association, and preside at the Female Prayer Meeting, be "at home" to calls, at all hours of the day, and of the most unmerciful length, from the very ones, perhaps, who will go away and wonder that Mrs. ——'s floors were not cleaner, or her work out of the way in better season; or "*did* you see that hole in Mr. ——'s coat?" "Yes, and Carrie's dress wanted mending sadly, and Willie's hands and face were really *dirty*. How *can* Mrs. —— *be so careless?*" And they know at the same time, that there is no hand but hers to do these things. How *is* she to do them, if each caller stays an hour or more? If a lady calls at ten o'clock on a minister's wife, who does her own work, because she has not the means to hire it done—can't she recollect that a dinner is to be prepared—that, possibly, while she sits idly chatting, the bread may be growing sour or burning. *When is* the floor to be scrubbed, or the work done, or the ragged coat or dress mended? Look in after ten o'clock at night, and you will see her finishing off the large wash, which you so thoughtlessly delayed; or still later, with aching head and weary frame, repairing the worn garments you so cruelly criticised. No wonder that the head is sick, and the whole heart faint, and at length, she, who only a few years ago came among them, fresh and hopeful, is laid to rest by the side of many who have been as needlessly sacrificed; or, what, to a sensitive spirit, is worse than dying, her husband is compelled, in order to save her life, to abandon a field of great and increasing usefulness, and remove her to her native land.

But Mrs. Herbert's heart was strong and hopeful, too fully engrossed in *present* labor, to indulge in dark forebodings for the future, and no leisure, to afflict herself by imagining what trials it might possibly bring.

Elder Blake and his wife, with whom they continued to board, were exceedingly attentive, and with their charges there could be no complaint. They received them into their house from kindness, and not with the hope of gain. Still Mary was quite confident that, could they once manage to meet the *first expenses* of *beginning*, they could, in a home of their own, no matter how humble, live even more economically, and the necessity for the most rigid caution, was becoming more and more evident each day. Mr. Herbert fully agreed with his wife on this point; but how could they raise the needful for the first, absolutely necessary, outlays. That was a problem which they could not solve. But Providence settled that question for them, about three months after their arrival, very unexpectedly.

Mr. Herbert was absent at a Presbytery meeting, when circumstances made it exceedingly desirable that Mrs. Blake should resume possession of the room they occupied. Mrs. Herbert could procure no other boarding-place, and, therefore, "a necessity was laid upon them" to commence housekeeping immediately, and Mary at once devoted herself to the novel labor of "house-hunting," and before one day expired, found it a much more laborious undertaking than she had anticipated.

Houses, and parts of houses, were plenty, but the rent was so far above their limited means, that there was no occasion for a moment's deliberation. She wearied herself going from house to house, looking into all imaginable and unimaginably filthy places, called tenements, but the same difficulty extended even to these. Her ideas of what *must* be had, were becoming more and more unpretending, with each new trial, until she was satisfied that anything under cover, which would protect them from rain and cold, and give place for a bed, stove, and her husband's books and study-table, would be gratefully received.

When hope was nearly exhausted, she was told one morning of some empty rooms, in the second-story of an old ungainly house, which might possibly be obtained. The lower story was owned and occupied by one of their church members, who, out of kindness to his pastor, would be inclined to place the rent within their reach. Mary hastened to examine, and if practicable, arrange for immediate possession.

One of her letters to Hill Farm, will give a more graphic description of this week's trials and experience, than any effort of mine could do.

"GLENVILLE, *Nov.* —, 18—.

"MY DEAR HOME FRIENDS:

"You will be surprised to learn that we

have relinquished our boarding plans, and are really settled in our own *home*—the most improbable of all events, when I last wrote. I can hardly realize now, that it is anything more than one of my day dreams.

"Shall I go back a few weeks and give you a short history of my 'life and adventures?'

"Circumstances which they could not control, made it necessary that Mr. and Mrs. Blake, with whom we have been boarding, should have possession of the room we have occupied since we came. George was from home when Mrs. Blake gave me this information, and I saw it was important for her, that we should make some change, as soon as possible. Both Mr. and Mrs. Blake have been exceedingly kind—a brother and sister could not have been more so.

"No other boarding-place, within the limit of our means, could be procured, and I commenced at once the new work of 'house-hunting.' I imagined it would be a very easy, and rather pleasant occupation; but I assure you, long before night, I changed my mind.

"Tenements were plenty enough, but the rent was far above my comprehension. A *house*, I supposed, I must have of course. A *small one*, to be sure, but how could we do without a kitchen, dining-room and parlor? Two chambers and a study were accommodations absolutely necessary.

"There was, however, a change of several degrees in my estimate of the 'must haves,' long ere I had finished my second day's search. I returned to my room wearied and perplexed, but by no means discouraged. You know, dear father, how often you have teased me for the pertinacity with which I always held on to a plan, or idea, and many times, I doubt not, it has been something of an annoyance to you, and perhaps other friends, especially, when my train of thoughts or wishes was at variance with their own. I certainly have always been accustomed to look upon it as a fault in my character. But 'that night could not the king sleep.' As I lay thinking and planning, the thought flashed across my mind—perhaps that very tenacity of thought and purpose, which in my girlhood-days, seemed an undesirable trait, may after all, help to carry me through many a strait place, and I suspect, *if it be a* characteristic needed for my present position, I shall find full employment for it all, and perhaps by it be able to add to, instead of detracting from, the comfort of those I love.

"You would smile, dear mother, if you knew how much this self-congratulatory train of thought comforted me in my perplexities. So much so, that I concluded to defer any further attempts at *reformation, till I had, at least, obtained a dwelling-placc.* After that I will take the matter again into consideration; but there is something so very refreshing in imagining that a youthful defect may, in riper years, be transformed into a most important and valuable quality, that I may not find it easy to return to my early, and more humble estimate of myself.

"I will not ask you to pardon this digression, for I please myself with the idea, that those to to whom I write, will like best to feel that my thoughts come to them, just as unconstrainedly as they would if I sat in your midst.

"After many hours' careful thought, I came to the conclusion that I was altogether too *aristocratic*, in my notions. Why had I not learned that a more primitive mode of house-keeping was, by far, the most desirable? The less room I had to care for, the more time I should have to be out among our people, and to carry out many plans, formed for helping George in various ways. Of course I must do my own work, and I would keep my kitchen so nice, that he would not object to taking our meals in it, especially, if I should be so fortunate as to find a place with a little shed attached, where I could put a stove, and do my rough work. Then the bed-room could be used for a study. A parlor and spare room would complete the list. Oh! yes, *four rooms* were all I could ask. Indeed, I rather thought I *wouldn't have more if I could!* This conclusion was a great relief, and pleasing myself with imagining how carefully the rooms were to be kept, and what a pleasant spot I would make it for my husband, I slept sweetly the few hours that remained for rest.

"The next morning I consulted with kind Deacon Blake, as to where I should be most likely to find that which I now sought. I could see plainly that he was pleased to find that my own judgment had decided on less room than I, at first, considered indispensable. Forty dollars per year, was all I dared to appropriate for rent; and oh! mother, if you could see all the places I looked into that weary day! Why, father's cattle would refuse to occupy them, till they had received many repairs; and yet no four, of even such rooms, could be obtained for forty dollars.

"When I returned to my boarding-place, I was 'fully persuaded in my own mind' that my 'stick-to-a-tiveness,' as Harry used to call it, *was no fault*, but one of the cardinal virtues, of which, I began to fear, I had not more than half enough; for I must own I retired to rest, as nearly discouraged as I ever remember to have been in my life.

"As I was preparing to renew my search the next morning, Deacon Blake informed me, with some hesitation, that perhaps Mr. Dudley could accommodate us with rooms over one of his buildings. I saw he was rather doubtful as to their being desirable, but I was very '*humble*' by this time.

"My paper warns me to close, and, like some of our fashionable periodicals, I will leave you in the midst of my story, and give you a rest till my next, which shall be forwarded as soon as my *household cares* will allow.

"With love ever bright and steadfast,

"Your affectionate child,

"M. HERBERT."

"GLENVILLE, *Nov.* —, 18—.

"MY DEAREST MOTHER:

"Of course I imagine you all impatience to learn the *finale* of my adventures, and I am quite as anxious to give them, that you may sooner be able to picture to yourselves our present situation.

"I went at once to Mr. Dudley, and found the rooms had for a long time been used, simply, as lumber rooms for the store adjoining. They were in the second story, Mr. Dudley's family occupying the main building. He 'doubted if they would suit; but here was the key; the lumber had all been removed, and I could examine for myself. The rent would be forty dollars.'

"I was glad to make the survey without witnesses; and, taking the key, I mounted the stairs. They were low, and easy of ascent. That was encouraging, at any rate. With a beating heart I entered, and closing the door, stood in blank dismay, in the middle of the room. Were these dismal, horridly dirty rooms to be our home? No, no; never! and my first impulse was to leave, without a second look. But if not *here*, *where* was I to look for anything better? I had hunted, faithfully, every part of the town, and this was the only spot I had found that I could, with any justice, think of appropriating. It would do no harm to examine these rooms carefully, and endeavor to think calmly, and decide honestly, uninfluenced by what others thought indispensable, or what I had been accustomed to think so. Now was the time, if ever, to follow my dear mother's example, and look 'only on the bright side.'

"The first room was quite large; but, oh, so filthy! But, patience, a good scrubbing-brush, plenty of soap and water, and a strong arm, aided by a cheerful, willing heart, could make wonderful changes in a few hours. The walls were bare, smoke-stained, and smeared with tobacco; a few coats of whitewash could cover all impurities. The floors were uneven, and badly spotted. We could not think of carpets; but surely Mr. Dudley would paint the floors and repair the broken hearth.

"There was a good closet in one corner, and a cupboard in the other. That was certainly a comfort.

"Things were looking brighter. I passed into the next room. It was of the same size, but so immeasurably dirtier, that the first became, by comparison, quite passable. But I must compel myself to hope, that the same remedies of patience, scrubbing-brush and soap, would 'hide a multitude of sins,' even here.

"A better hearth than the first room could boast, with an opening over the mantel for stove-pipe—a closet, with shelves covered with a combination of stains and dirt, which no chemical skill could have separated or analyzed, and a rickety sink, might, by a stretch of imagination, be classed under the *comforts*, in this forlorn survey. However, the *two other rooms* may be in a better condition. I will not allow my courage to fail, until I have seen the whole. But where are they?

"There was, indeed, a door in the back room, but it was nailed up, and peering through the key-hole, I found it opened into the lumber loft of the store adjoining.

"The hall through which I entered into the two rooms under deliberation, divided them from Mrs. Dudley's chambers, and there could be, of course, no other apartments in this story. *Four* rooms had appeared so absolutely necessary, that I had never imagined it possible to do with less. But others, it seemed, had thought *two* might be made to answer. Here was a good opportunity to examine my '*high notions*' (an expression I had accidentally heard used of myself, only the day before), and see if they were capable of further pruning.

"In no enviable state of mind, I paced to and fro many times across this very 'Dismal Swamp,' earnestly endeavoring to see in what way I could contrive, by the utmost exertion of Yankee ingenuity, to make such a *den* inhabitable, or *two* rooms at all sufficient for comfort. If it was only for *myself*—but pride and affection both rebelled, when I thought of my husband. I did feel that he deserved something better; and cramped and uncomfortable apartments seem so much worse for a man, than for a woman, especially if he is one whose occupation calls for mental labor, that my whole soul revolted. But rebellious thoughts were at once checked by the perpetually recurring question: If not here, *where* else can you turn?

"I paused a moment to look out of the window, hoping, gloomy as was the prospect *within*, there might be cheer and amusement in the outward surroundings. But wretchedly muddy streets, lined with very common-looking business houses, were all the comfort that the front view presented. The rear opened into a back yard, quite spacious enough for a handsome garden. But no such blessing met the eye. It was a dirty yard, full of mud-holes, with bits of staves, old barrel hoops, broken crockery, worn-out brooms, strips of scrub-cloths, pieces of shoes, brimless hats, and every description of rubbish or lumber, scattered all abroad. A large well, with an old-fashioned curb and windlass, stood in the centre. The yard itself was a kind of *court*, inclosed by *tenement* houses on three sides, into which the *spouts* of *all* the sinks of both upper and lower stories emptied. The fourth side was barricaded by an old and much dilapidated barn, and beyond this court—well, we won't speak of the 'Five Points' looking lanes beyond!

"Was not this cheering? I was glad to turn back again to the interior. One more look, and with a sigh I descended, and asked Mr. Dudley for the refusal of the rooms, till I could consult my husband.

"I then alluded to the repairs, but was told that for our sakes, he had placed the rent so *low*, he could put no expense upon the rooms. So I returned to my boarding-place (which never looked half so pleasant before), to make arrangements to go to George, the next morning. He was at a meeting in a neighboring city, the one where he had finished his preparatory education, and had been absent two weeks. The captain of a boat, which passed daily between Glenville and that place, would, I knew, cheerfully give me a free passage to my husband. A sleepless night, and the sail up the river, the next morning, gave me abundant time for undisturbed meditation.

"My chief anxiety was that George would object, peremptorily, to the thought of such an arrangement, and by the time I reached the city, I had contrived so many ways by which the *rooms* could be improved, that now to abandon the idea, would have been a real disappointment. Beside, *I* knew, as *he* could not, without passing through my last week's experience, how hopeless was the attempt to find anything more desirable. My courage had risen with that knowledge—and now the hope of 'bringing light out of such darkness, and order from such confusion,' was quite exhilarating.

"My husband was greatly surprised when he saw me, and you may be sure, still more so when he learned my errand. The thought of but two rooms did not trouble him in the least, and his opinion of the capabilities of any one trained by you, dear mother, is so exalted, that the extreme filthiness of the place gave him no uneasiness.

"'But, my dear Mary,' said he, 'what are we to do for the furnishing? I have no doubt but you will make two rooms, or even *one*, a pleasant home, and am quite sure that all under your care will be sweet and clean; but, great as is my confidence in your abilities, I cannot believe that even your ingenuity can make "brick without straw," or procure the simplest articles for housekeeping with an empty purse.'

"My husband's brother Frank, and his bride, were with us, listening with much amusement to our conversation, and he said, laughingly;

"'Ah! George, you have asked a question, now, which my hopeful sister will find some trouble in answering. Will you not, Mary?'

"'It *is* a strong argument against the arrangement I advocate, I acknowledge; but the change proposed is not of our seeking. There is a "*necessity laid upon us.*" We *cannot* find a boarding-place. We *cannot* live in the streets—we *must not* embarrass ourselves with debt.

"'But, "where there is a will, Providence will open a way." If we strive to help ourselves, and are content with the most simple accommodations, I am confident God will assist us. I confess I do not see *how*, as yet, very clearly; but am so sure of it—that I sincerely believe we ought to go forward, "nothing doubting."'

"'It would be wicked to throw obstacles in the way of such faith and courage,' said our kind brother. 'Allow Kate and myself to aid you in taking the first step. Who knows but it may prepare the way for a second. We would be most happy to present you with a cooking stove—*that* being a very important article in house-keeping; unless you prefer the more primitive mode of making your coffee—boiling your potatoes—frying your ham—and feeding your pig—all in one skillet, as I have often seen done in these regions. But our gift is encumbered with one proviso, which may render it valueless.'

"'Name it. I do not fear to accept any conditions our kind brother can make.'

"'You are rash, sister dear. But the only return I ask is that my wife and I shall be your first invited guests whenever your plans are fairly completed.'

"'Oh, thank you—thank you. The visit will only increase our indebtedness—nothing, *not even the stove*, could gratify us more, for you know sister Kate and myself are almost twin sisters.'

"'Well, Mary, one step is taken. Let's hear what is to be the next, for your tell-tale eyes assure me you see light ahead; though I confess, I cannot find my way one inch beyond brother's stove.'

"'To whom do the few articles in the room you occupied in the seminary, belong?'

"A hearty laugh was my first reply.

"'Oh, sister Mary, did you ever go into that room,' said Kate. 'Have you the faintest idea that those things can, by any skill, be made useful? A woefully infirm table, three chairs still worse, and one, I believe, minus a leg, for I tried it once to my sorrow, and the bed!'

"'If,' said my husband, laughing, 'it has been in the room ever since I vacated it, I'll engage it is already claimed by occupants, whose name is *Legion*, and the mattress is far more unfit for use. Except my bookcases, or rather boxes, there is no one thing in that room that can be good for aught but kindling-wood, else I should not have left them there. You may take my word for that, my dear.'

"'No, no, George, not even your word should deter me from trying what can be done. If I had faith to see those rooms which I have told you of transformed, I need not doubt but we shall be able to purify anything. If you will engage your old washwoman, to take the articles into the Seminary-yard, and do her best toward cleansing them, I will try to perfect her labors myself, when we get them to Glenville. Capt. James has promised to land all we may wish to send, and ourselves, at the wharf, close by *our home*, without charge. Thus, you see, this may prove another step, and if you will be willing to purchase the stove to-day, which Frank kindly offers, and hasten our arrangements as much as possible, I imagine we shall find our light shining brighter and brighter, as we proceed; I long to show our good brother and sister how short a time it will take to make your old things look 'ain maist as weel as new,' and also to convince them that it takes but a very, very little to make a pleasant home.'

"'But, sister mine,' said Kate, 'what are the prospects for crockery, beds (for your *treasure* is only a single bed), kitchen utensils, etc?'

"'I'll show you,' replied my husband, taking out his purse, and holding up fifty cents.

"'As Mary has made arrangements for our passage home, she shall have what was to have paid mine, toward her house furnishing. That's every cent in prospect, for six weeks to come. Say, May bird, have you a magic ring, that will multiply this little bit of silver into gold, or bank-bills, sufficient for our present need?'

"In reply, I laid into his hand thirty dollars in gold! What a look!

"'*Where* in the wide world did you get this, Mary, and how?'

"'*Honestly*, my good husband, if you will allow me to answer your last question first, for you look very much as if you feared I had been *pilfering*. You must not look grave, however, when I tell you all about it. You know, I have never used the handsome cloak father gave me, just before we left New England. My shawl and travelling cloak are more in keeping with our present means. I know father would rather I sold it, for a good price, than be in debt for a moment. Mrs. Turner wanted the *cloak*, and *I* wanted the *money*, so we *swapped*. How could a Yankee help it when so good an opportunity offered?

And now, my good sister, do you not see that we shall do "excellently well?"'

"We were to dine at Gov. Roberts', an old and tried friend of George's, and Frank insisted that we should stop and purchase the stove on the way; which we accordingly did, to the entire satisfaction of all concerned.

"At the dinner-table, Kate entertained our friends with some account of our morning's discussions, and, though I did not think of it at the time, I suspect the kind-hearted girl had a benevolent object in view, for on leaving, Mrs. Roberts took me up to her attic, saying, she wished for the pleasure of lending a helping hand, and gave me a bureau, a pair of brass andirons, shovel and tongs, with which, said she, 'I began housekeeping, more than forty years ago.'

"My heart was so full I could not speak. All the darkness and uncertainty fled from before such unexpected kindness, and, like Joseph of old, I wished for some 'place where to weep,' for very gladness. Nor was this all. When we parted, my kind friend said, 'Let me claim a mother's privilege, and advise you to rest the remainder of the afternoon, and leave all other arrangements for to-morrow, because I think Mrs. Watson and Mrs. Reeves (two ladies who dined with us, and old friends of George's) are intending to send you a package in the evening. It is possible it may contain some things you would think best to purchase, were you to go shopping on your way back to your brother's boarding place.'

"There was little danger of our doing much in *that line*, but I felt her kindness none the less, and left her with warm thanks and love.

"As we passed beyond the gate, Frank smilingly inquired: 'What could have transpired while you and good Mrs. Roberts were up-stairs? Your eyes were so full of tears, as you returned, I should have suspected you had been annoyed in some way, were it not for the smile on your lips. So I hope you have taken step number three, toward our visit. You see how selfish I am.'

"I informed them of my increasing riches—and also that Mrs. Roberts would send them all to the landing, on the morrow, and perhaps meet us there, to say good bye.

"The articles from the other ladies—to which Mrs. Roberts alluded—came, just as our lamps were lighted, after tea, and our good friends would have had no doubt of our appreciation of their kindness, could they have seen the pleasure with which they were examined.

"There were two good woollen blankets, a new comforter—one white spread, and a pretty patch-work. Two pairs of sheets and pillow cases, two table-cloths and half dozen napkins and towels. A half dozen knives and forks. Some German silver spoons—an old fashioned Britannia tea and water pot, in excellent condition, and quite neat in style—a pair of plated candle-stick snuffers and tray, etc. etc.

"Verily our cup runneth over, and we, surely, shall not want for any good thing.

"When the survey was completed. Sister Kate remarked, 'I must say this looks exceedingly like an early invitation to Glenville—and I shall be all anxiety, to see you on board to-morrow, that you may expedite your renovating, and purifying plans, and thus hasten our advent, for I shall not rest till I see this new home, and judge for myself of your success.'

"I will not linger longer, my dear friends. It is all so new and interesting to me, that I forget that I may be making my narrative very tedious to you. In my next I will but give you a few more items—and introduce you to *our home*,

"Till then, farewell,

"Lovingly, yours always,

"M. Herbert."

CHAPTER VI.

AT HOME.

OUR friends found Mrs. Roberts at the boat when they reached it, with a large hamper of groceries—tea, coffee, sugar, and spices; several jars of sweetmeats, a box of butter, some hams, soap and starch, etc., just for a beginning; and as she said "good bye," she left a note in Mary's hand, which, on opening, contained twenty-five dollars, and these words: "A love-token, from one who has long esteemed you for your husband's sake, and is now sure to do so for your own."

Who ever felt so rich as our young couple? They had written and engaged the rooms the day before, and on landing went at once to see them, and take the preparatory steps for cleaning and furnishing them.

Mr. Herbert was evidently not prepared for the worst, and had no faith that any labor could make them decent. But it was now too late for repining—it was Wednesday morning, or rather almost noon, and they were determined to be "settled" by Saturday night.

Brushes, soap and whitewash were procured, and they both went to work "with a will." The gentleman was, at first, a little awkward in the use of the brush, but Mary found him, on the whole, a most able and docile pupil.

They went over the rooms many, many times, before the most disgusting stains could be obliterated. But patient industry can accomplish wonders, and soon the walls began to look almost white, and the wood-work disclose the original color of the paint.

"If we could only get this floor painted it would save us time, and much hard scrubbing." And George determined to see Mr. Dudley, and endeavor to persuade him to have it done. "No." "Well, then, we will do it ourselves." "No, no," his idea was that floors were *injured by paint*, and he never allowed it on any of his tenements!

"Never mind," said Mary, when her husband told her the result of the application; "there is this comfort, it will be growing better all the time, and I doubt not, a few weeks' care will make it quite white and free from stains. A *carpet* now, would be quite an institution; but, as we *can't* have one, we'll just imagine that carpets are as injurious as brother Dudley considers paint to be."

Well, it is Saturday morning, all must be in order by noon, that the young housekeepers may sit down to their first meal in their "own hired" rooms, and feel that there is nothing to interfere with the enjoyment of the Sabbath.

Mr. Herbert's books have been carefully dusted, their cases washed and polished, and he has arranged them, while Mary, with various kinds of purifying lotions, has been busy over the college articles, in the back yard.

The old mattress had been taken to pieces, the hair carefully washed and picked, a new tick provided, and the whole reconstructed by good mother Reed, in whom Mary had been so much interested at her first interview. A young carpenter had volunteered to repair the broken chairs, and furnishing Mrs. Herbert with the material, she had varnished her simple furniture herself.

The last touches have been given, and the young wife puts on a neat wrapper and prepares the table for dinner. Friends from among their people have so bountifully supplied her with all manner of food, that she will have little opportunity to display her own skill for some days to come.

She carefully surveys her table when all is ready, her smile betokening great satisfaction, and then throws open the door into the front room, where her husband, having finished his task, stands, with glistening eyes, admiring its tidy and already homelike appearance. He meets her as she enters, and passing his arm fondly around her waist, whispers, "My own Mary, can this comfortable abode be the same we looked upon not four days since?"

But we will step aside and leave Mrs. Herbert to describe its present appearance:

"GLENVILLE, *Nov.* 28, 18—.

"MY DEAR MOTHER:

"If you could only look in upon us now! It is our *first evening* '*at home.*' George is before his study table preparing for to-morrow's (Sabbath) duties, and I sit at one side, with so much to tell, yet almost too happy to write.

"You have not forgotten my description of

these rooms, as I first saw them—and I want you to bear it in mind, as I proceed. I closed my last letter with the account of our finished arrangements to leave the city, and return to Glenville."

(It is not necessary to repeat, what has already been told—so we drop that part of the letter—and begin with her description of the present appearance of the place.)

"And now, my dear friends, please follow me, once more, into this front room. Make yourselves perfectly at home—and use your eyes as freely as you choose. No fear that I shall consider it impertinent curiosity.

"Where shall I begin to show you the glories of my house. With its chief joy, I think—my *husband.* Look at him, my mother—as he sits in that comfortable study-chair—his whole mind intent upon the subject before him. May I not be proud of him, if I hide it deep in my own heart—where none, but the dear home friends, can see it? Is he not one to lean upon, and trust in every emergency? May I not be assured that all my imperfections will be met with kindness, gentleness, and forbearance? So far, it has been so, even beyond my wildest hopes—and who can look at him, and fear any change? Will it not be easy to encounter trials and deprivations, or rather will they not cease to be such, in the endeavor to create a happy home for him?

"But I must not forget politeness to my guests, or linger by his side, just now.

"How do you like this study-table, Harry? Is it not 'just the thing!' I varnished it myself, and covered the top with that nice, black cloth. Almost too good for the purpose, do you say, dear mother? But do not accuse me of extravagance. It is not new—nor is it the 'skirt of Saul's coat;' but a piece which I found in my husband's dilapidated wardrobe.

"And what think you of this new fashioned bookcase, fastened to the back of the table? It is a discarded dish closet, which the last occupant of this room had thrown into the back yard, as utterly worthless. George nailed together the broken parts and painted it, and now I think it looks quite stylish.

"The long boxes made expressly to pack books in—when Mr. Herbert first came West, to finish his education—have been well scoured, varnished, and now, set one atop the other, open side out and filled with the books purchased by his own labors while in college, make, I am sure you will say, very imposing bookcases.

"In the middle of the room, you perceive, we have a few yards of cotton carpeting, which were found in the famous bundle given us, by the kind friends, of whom I told you in my last.

"It is not ornamental, but will save quite a good deal of scrubbing.

"A simple, stained bed-stead, comes next in order, with its *husk* mattress, and *pillows* of the same material (*feathers*, you know, are enervating —but this is cool and healthful), and the pure white spread, give it quite a *genteel* air, which last is of marvellous importance to our peace of mind.

"Next, dear kind Mrs. Roberts' bureau—all that we need, and with containing powers of almost unlimited capacity. A fifty cent glass is quite large enough to show us our faces once a day —and being a little hazy and uneven, we shall have no temptation to a needless expenditure of time.

"That pretty, simple, work stand, in the corner, dear mother, is a present from George; bought with the little *gold badge of his college society*.

"These large, bright andirons, shovel and tongs, are almost too magnificent, beside our other furnishing; but we are grateful for them, notwithstanding, and should miss them sadly, if they were withdrawn, not only for their usefulness, but because they remind us so much of the dear old parlor at 'Hill Farm.'

"A clock, two plated candlesticks, snuffer and tray, and a brass lamp, which has lighted my husband's studies ever since he was in college, are our mantel ornaments, and four new wooden-seated chairs and a pine dining-table, complete the list of the furniture in this, our principal room. In the cupboard, may be seen a neat set of white ware (not ample—but answering all our wants and leaving some spare pieces for such guests as can be content with few changes), a Britannia tea and water-pot and our German silver spoons. The little closet, behind the study table, has abundant room for my small stock of bed and table linen.

"This room, you will perceive, is parlor, study, dining-room, bed-chamber, and anything else we may find it necessary to call it.

"Let me introduce you, now, to the adjoining apartment.

"And first, brother Frank's gift, *our stove*, with all its bright tin furnishing; second, the despised college and seminary bedstead, in the far corner, shining with fresh paint and varnish, and rejoicing in a new, or rather, a clean mattress. I have put some curtains around it, of fourpenny calico, which was, with other blessings, in Mrs. Robert's basket. It looks like a simple curtained bed, does it not? Look behind the curtains and learn what it is, when not put to its legitimate use. By the garments pinned to that strong band around the top, you perceive it can be converted easily into a wardrobe, for clothes-closets are not *fashionable* here. *On* the bed, are the bonnet and hat-boxes, clothes-basket, etc.; and *underneath*, our trunks, packed with such articles as are not for immediate use.

"Now, say you'll remain with us through the night, and see how quickly these articles will be folded and placed in the basket, and put with the trunks—out of sight—and the bed prepared for ourselves, while we give you possession of study, parlor, and bed-chamber. Surely no guest can wish for more ample accommodation.

"The closet for kitchen utensils; the three old chairs, made new by paint; the sink, with a new leg and spout, the cracks filled with putty and neatly painted, and a cover which can be buttoned back, when the sink is needed, or let down and used as an ironing or bread board, at suitable times; *these* need no explanation. But can you guess what is hidden in this angle of the room, under a curtain of that same cheap calico? Look! overhead, a wooden bar is nailed, as you perceive, across which are hung a saddle, bridle, buffalo-skin, and a pair of saddle-bags, which have been given my husband for travelling. (Don't look for the *horse* there, Johnny; George must borrow that when he goes to Presbytery meetings.) Under these, on the floor, you see a barrel of flour, one of potatoes, washtubs, clothes-boiler, and a box of soap. Garret, cellar, and store-closet all in one. Who can be so unreasonable as to ask for more room? Not I.

"Thus, my dear ones, we are fairly at housekeeping, provided with everything necessary for comfort, and a few dollars left in the purse, to make us feel *independent.* We have now *begun life* for ourselves. How much toil, sickness, and sorrow are before us, it is well we cannot foresee, and it would be folly to make the attempt. We have only *one day* at a time to live, and with cheerful courage, unswerving love and confidence in each other, and trust in God, we can, surely, meet all that each day brings. Therefore, dear mother, do not be anxious for your children. I cannot, nor can you, expect my life will be all sunshine; but I do believe, if I do my duty, I shall find quite as much of real happiness as those whom the world calls rich.

"We shall this evening send our invitation to brother Frank and wife, for I long, exceedingly, to show them how pleasantly and comfortably we are situated.

"Good night. With earnest love for you all,

"YOUR MARY."

Early the next week, the brother and sister made the promised visit. Mrs. Herbert was an entire stranger to all her husband's family; but the extremely pleasant interview with these two friends, while making their present arrangements, had prepared her to expect great enjoyment from this reunion.

And four happier persons the sun seldom shines upon, than are now gathered in this neat and simple home. The brothers are congenial spirits, knit together, like David and Jonathan, in the strongest affection. Frank is taller and more slender than George, with less appearance of robust health; but still, the resemblance between the brothers is very striking, in character as well as personal appearance. Both are heartily devoted to the work in which they are engaged. Both exhibit, in a very uncommon degree, great earnestness and manliness, with almost womanly delicacy and gentleness. A combination rarely met with, but exceedingly precious when found.

Never was there a greater contrast than the sisters—Kate was considerably above the medium height. A fine figure, easy and dignified manners, and glossy black hair, sufficient to wrap her as in a mantle, fine open brow, eyes black as night, beautifully tender in her softer moods, but flashing grandly, if wrong was to be redressed, or a noble deed performed. Highly educated, and nurtured in affluence, she will be an invaluable, intellectual companion for her husband, more so than Mary, but probably not as capable of patient endurance, or physical exertion.

Mary's figure was larger, and not so graceful or dignified, and her educational advantages had been far inferior. She was inclined to grieve over this, fearing that she might not prove, in all things, such a wife as her loving heart believed her husband must deserve. Her ardent desire for a thorough education had caused her to place, perhaps, too light an estimate on domestic qualifications, while she imagined that talent, and a high order of intellect, were indispensably requisite for a clergyman's wife.

Her hair was of a dark chestnut, folded neatly round a well-shaped head, with a low brow, blue eyes, and clear, rosy complexion. As her husband marks the affectionate greeting, and loving earnestness, with which she receives her guests, his eyes rest tenderly upon her, and no one can doubt, but he, at least, is abundantly satisfied.

"Why, sister mine," said Kate, as she was placed in a most comfortable easy-chair, "this is altogether too luxurious. I thought there was to be nothing but the simplest and most absolute necessaries. I fear I shall be obliged to lecture you upon extravagance, at the very beginning."

"First hear my defence, most gracious lady. You are seated in that old arm-chair, found in my husband's bachelor sanctum, which you assured me was only fit for burning. George has made a high back to it by nailing on a board, and I have stuffed it into shape, and covered it with an old dress, too short for me, found in that inexhaustible basket of mother Roberts. Am I acquitted, madam?"

"Most fully," said Kate, rising. "But don't think I am going to sit still, before you have shown me all over your premises."

"That will not occupy much time," replied George, opening the door between the two rooms; "but, I doubt if you will find more true comfort in the abodes of wealth, or more grateful hearts than are contained in these two homely rooms."

The survey was made, great pleasure expressed, enlivened by many sportive and affectionate remarks, and then Mary excused herself to prepare for dinner.

These "simple annals" may prove tiresome to my readers, and perhaps I linger foolishly; but there is something inexpressibly sweet in recalling incidents connected with the earlier life of these four young friends. Very dear were they all to my heart, and many times, in after years, have I seen Mary's care-worn face light up with almost the freshness of its bridal bloom, as she recalled for her children the pleasures of her earliest experiments in house-keeping, and these narrations always closed with the assertion, that no part of her married life was so distinctly fixed in memory as that first visit from Frank and Kate.

Life, to those who then assembled around that neat and generous board, was full of most cheerful anticipations. They knew that sorrow and disappointment was common to all; but why need they dread them, while hoping to labor and endure together?

"*Sorrow and disappointment*," were vague terms to them in these bright days. It takes *experience* to give them a definite meaning. Happy are those who do not seek to understand the future, till the Providence of God unfolds it, and at the same time gives the strength and grace to endure whatever it may bring.

CHAPTER VII.

MRS. REED'S HISTORY.

SOME three months have flown rapidly away. Little has passed to disturb the quiet happiness of our friends. A few trials, such as are common to all faithful pastors, have fallen upon Mr. Herbert, but in general, his labors have been uncommonly acceptable, and his audience so increased, as to make the little church uncomfortably full—a state of things unknown before.

Some have held off to see whereunto this will grow—a few prophets of evil affirmed that two or three months more would suffice to exhibit all the new preacher's "college learning" and then—but the community, as a whole, were satisfied that Mr. Herbert would become more and more popular and useful as months pass by.

Mary, of course, found her share of trials—more, perhaps, than her husband—of those *little* things which sting like nettles, and yet make one ashamed of the consciousness that such trifles have any power to vex or annoy. It is a curious fact, that fault-finding parishioners are generally too cowardly to attack a clergyman himself, and therefore when they wish to show their displeasure and punish him, they contrive to do it by throwing trifling vexations in the way of his wife. But, if the husband, either through misjudged, or unguarded friendships, or through fear of his people, is ever tempted to listen to these petty words of censure or complaint from others, then woe be to that wife! It is an evil which creeps upon a man insidiously, but it will nevertheless undermine all true happiness, and, when once admitted, there is no escape in life. The grave is the only refuge from the sorrow which will surely flow from it, and happy is she who in such circumstances, is early permitted to repose therein. In the present case, however, while each maintained full confidence in the other, there was little danger of serious harm from such attacks.

Mary soon learned that it would be impossible for their salary to support them, even with the most rigid economy. That their church did all they could, for the present, they had no reason to doubt.

But some way must be devised to add a trifle, at least, to their means. She had not uninterrupted leisure sufficient to teach, even if the place could furnish pupils, without withdrawing them from those who needed the income still more than they did. Sewing was the only way opened, and to that Mr. Herbert, at first, resolutely objected. Not long, however, for he could not but see the necessity for it, and, before spring, they were indebted to his wife's nimble fingers, for many comforts.

She would have grieved had her mother known that her longed-for home letters, were often detained in the office till she could earn the twenty-five cents (postage at that time) with which to release them, or that she had sewed late into the night, to procure their dinner the next day. This last, not often, however, for provisions were, for the most part, abundant, and fabulously cheap.

One stormy afternoon in February Mr. Herbert came home and asked his wife if she thought it would be safe for her to venture out to see Mrs. Reed, who was considered dangerously ill. Mrs. Herbert made no delay in preparing for the walk, for their first acquaintance had matured into strong affection, and the fear of losing this dear friend was exceedingly painful.

They found Mrs. Reed rapidly sinking, and Dr. Strong, who was present, felt that she would probably pass away before morning. She had long been feeble, though she never complained; but was ever busy for herself or others. Mr. and Mrs. H. were greatly surprised, therefore, when the physician informed them that he had known for months that she was in a hopeless condition, and she had also been fully aware of it, herself.

Mrs. Herbert decided, at once, to remain and watch with her friend, and the patient sufferer's look of affectionate gratitude, was reward sufficient, had any been needed. After a prayer, her husband returned home, leaving her to make such arrangements as were necessary before Dr. Strong left.

The house was a miserable concern, and very destitute of comforts. Passing from the dingy and poorly ventilated sick-room, to the little shed, used for a kitchen, Mrs. Herbert was startled, almost beyond her self-control, by some dark object stretched before the door. Hastening back, she quietly beckoned the doctor outside. "What is that?" she whispered, fearfully. He bent over the object—"Oh, Pshaw! that's only old Reed, come home, as usual, drunk as a beast."

"Why! Dr. Strong, you astonish me. I have always supposed Mrs. Reed was a widow."

"Oh, no. If she were she might have been very differently situated. I understand, now, why the poor woman has failed so rapidly. He has, probably, just returned from one of his longest tramps, to wring from her more of her hard earnings. No wonder you thought her a widow. He leaves her, months at a time, and only comes back when he can no longer obtain money elsewhere to waste in debauchery. He has been gone now more than a year, and we all hoped that he would trouble her no more. The villain! he deserves hanging. But you, my dear madam, must return to our patient, or she will be troubled at your absence. I will meanwhile get some one to assist me in putting this miserable being aside for the night, where you will not be disturbed or alarmed by him."

"Poor Mrs. Reed!" said Mary, "when I first saw her, I thought there was an aching heart hidden beneath that gentle, subdued demeanor."

When she returned, she perceived that Mrs.

Reed understood her motive, in calling the doctor out; but not a word was spoken, alluding to it, till all directions were given for the night, and they were left alone. Then, taking Mrs. Herbert's hand, the invalid drew her to the bed-side, saying:

"Sit close by me; my voice is fast failing, and there is much that I wish to tell you if my strength will permit. If not taxing your kindness too severely, I desire to give you a short history of a sad, and very eventful life; it may help you to do good to others, when I have passed away.

"I was an only child—the cherished idol of my parents; reared in affluence, with no thought that a wish of mine could pass ungratified.

"I was but sixteen when I met Charles Reed, at a dancing party. Oh, could parents realize how much of sin and suffering originate in such assemblies, they would surely devise some less dangerous amusement for their loved ones. The simple act of dancing is as sinless as any exercise can be; it is the associations formed, the delirious excitement of music and the dance, and worse than all, the stimulating beverage so lavishly provided, that unfit the young for exercising discretion or judgment, or resisting temptations, which, in a calmer moment, amid the holy safeguards of home, would have no power to harm.

"I knew that Reed was not one whom my parents would countenance; but his person was faultless, and his manners far more attractive and polished than any young man's in my native place. He was poor, but that would have had no weight with my parents, had his habits and morals been without reproach.

"When first introduced to him, I knew that the community looked upon him as a gay, unprincipled man; but what harm could there be in conversing or dancing with him at a party, where the amusement of the present hour was all that was wished or intended?

"Young Reed was exceedingly popular, and in great demand at all the social gatherings among the young people, because of his remarkable ability to enliven and entertain his associates, and my parents knew that he was always present at all such amusements. It was ONLY IN THE QUIET HOME CIRCLE, where the mother's love and father's watchfulness are ever vigilant, to protect the young and innocent from danger, that he would have been refused admittance, and felt to be an unfit companion.

"I will not linger. Enough—we met often in *public* places, and soon my judgment was no longer consulted—*my heart* alone spoke; and oh, how wildly I loved that man! Had I not been infatuated, I should have indignantly discarded him forever, when, after winning an acknowledgment of my affection, his first request was, that I would consent to a clandestine marriage, fearing, as he averred, a refusal from my family on account of his poverty. But, thank God, I was saved that sin! My parents, when consulted, earnestly, and with great tenderness (but too late!) warned me of the danger, and entreated me to relinquish all idea of such a union. But, though I could not deny that my lover had been addicted to intemperance, gaming and other vices, yet I assured them he *had most certainly reformed* (in the short space of *three months*) and my love was to save him from a relapse!

"At length, with sad hearts, and many tears, my parents yielded, as my health was failing under their tender opposition, and we were married.

"My father furnished a house with great elegance, and placed a liberal sum in my husband's hands, that he might at once commence business free from all embarassment and with no temptation to go astray.

"Oh, how soon was I roused from my dream of bliss! Too impatient of the restraints he had submitted to for some months, to endure them after the victim—and, alas! that for which alone he valued her, the fortune—was in his power, my husband cast aside the mask the moment the marriage ceremony was solemnized.

"We left immediately for our bridal tour, with the promise of returning in two weeks, to take possession of our beautiful home. That home, furnished with so much care by my fond parents, I *never entered*, and from the hour my mother clasped her only child to her breast, in a tearful farewell, and my father, with quivering lips, blessed the young bride, I have never seen them! Thirty-five years of, oh how much sorrow and anguish!

"On our wedding-day, my father placed my fortune into my husband's hands, I having resolutely rejected his desire to settle a part of it on myself, and—can you believe such depravity possible—the house and furniture were disposed of to pay "debts of honor," even before that day—a *private* bargain, not to be disclosed, or take effect, till after we were gone!

"Not for *one day—our wedding day*—did he,

who had vowed before God and man to love and cherish me, retain the semblance of kindness. I was hurried South, and strictly watched by himself, and a creature of his will. All trace of our residence was carefully hidden from my parents, and for years we never heard, each of the other. When, at last, my fortune was all squandered, I was commanded to write to my father for another supply, and my obedience was insured by the promise, that if a certain sum was made over to my husband, I should, as soon as he received it, be allowed to leave him, and return to my precious home. The conditions were most joyfully complied with, on the part of my parents: but I was kept a closer prisoner than before.

"The next I heard, was of my parents' loss of property and death. My father had impoverished himself, at a time when all his available means were greatly needed, to meet a business crisis, in the vain hope of rescuing his child from a most cruel fate. The double failure broke his heart, and my gentle mother was laid to rest by his side the same week.

"When these facts were ascertained, and there was no longer, a hope of obtaining pecuniary aid through me, Mr. Reed brought me here, and left me destitute. I had no means to go home—and why should I wish to go, when those whose love consecrated the home, were not there to welcome me?"

Exhaustion and excitement compelled Mrs. Reed to interrupt this painfully interesting narrative, and, for many minutes, Mrs. Herbert stood over her friend, using every exertion to prevent convulsions, or fainting. When she became more composed, Mary begged she would make no further attempt to continue the history, till after a night's rest. With a sad, but very expressive smile, she replied: "Dear Mrs. Herbert, it must be told now, or never. I have but little more to add. Let me speak while I yet have the ability.

"For years I supported myself, and trusted I should be left in peace. But whenever he is on the verge of starvation, he returns, and despoils me of everything that he can dispose of. For the last ten years I have earnestly endeavored to lead a Christian life, and during that time have striven to forgive my husband for all the misery he has wrought, and also to reclaim him, if that be possible. It is this earnest desire, dear Mrs. Herbert, which has induced me to confide to your keeping a history, which should, otherwise, have been buried with me in the grave. I see great changes in this miserable man since his last return. His health, by so long a course of dissipation, has at length been entirely destroyed, and I do not feel that he can live long. You have been very kind to me, and to none, since I left my father's house, has my heart turned so lovingly, as to you and your noble husband. It seems cruel to requite all your attentions by this legacy of care and sorrow, and yet, dear friend, his soul is as precious as our own. Will you and Mr. Herbert watch over him, and try to lead him out of darkness into light, when I am gone? I see you shrink from it. His cruelty to me makes the thought repugnant. I can say little more. Life is fast ebbing—faster than I thought—but I must plead with you, for him still. Remember, great will be your reward."

"I accept your charge," said Mrs. Herbert, "most willingly. All that we can do to reclaim one so near to you shall be done. But do not talk of dying. My heart clings to you as to a mother in this strange land; and though I am ashamed to speak of trials, after your painful story, yet some there are, and more will follow, when I shall need your kind sympathy, and just such advice as, your long experience has prepared you to give. Our little church cannot spare you. You will soon be better, and God will give you to us, and all who love you, yet many days."

But even while she spoke, a strange shadow had settled on this dear friend's face, and her voice was broken and faint as she replied:

"No, my child. I have long expected this, and am, I trust, prepared, and more than willing to depart, and be with Jesus. The light of another earthly Sabbath will never shine for me, but I go to a brighter world—a perpetual Sabbath. To the land of peace and rest—to the holy Father, whose hand has led me by a way I knew not—to the blessed Saviour, who died that I might live. The footsteps of the welcome Messenger are even now on the threshold, the songs of the redeemed are ringing in my ears, angels are beckoning me, and the spirits of my earthly parents are saying, 'Come up hither.' I come. Farewell, my daughter. God ever bless"——

Mary sprang to her feet, and bent over the dying woman. Her eye beamed with a glorious light, speaking joy unutterable. One smile, borrowed from the angels hovering near her, and the patient, uncomplaining sufferer slept in Jesus.

With a strength not her own, Mrs. Herbert calmly closed her eyes, straightened the emaciated limbs, and folded on her breast those ever busy hands, whose "labor was now all o'er," and then knelt by the bedside alone with the dead.

When Mrs. Herbert rose from her prayer, it was still too dark to go for assistance, and she saw the necessity of acting by herself. Doubtful if in that poor abode things needful could be found, she opened a bureau, and carefully examined the wardrobe of her friend. She was turning away, unsuccessful, when, at the bottom of a drawer, she noticed a parcel, folded in a napkin of the finest damask. In this she found all the usual habiliments for the grave, snowy white, and prepared with the utmost neatness. The style of the articles, and the quality, impressed her at once with the certainty, that these were the remains of her bridal outfit, hoarded through all her poverty and deprivations, for this solemn occasion. There was something so sad, so touching in the thought, that the self-control, which had not wavered through all this trying night, forsook her, and she wept like a child.

Alone, in this noiseless midnight, did Mary array the poor, worn body in these mementoes of former affluence and withered hopes. Sadly and tearfully, as she arranged each garment, did her imagination fill up the brief history she had that night heard. Oh, it was a dark picture; but how many thousand just such are in our midst! Hearts are breaking all around us daily—won by loving words, which cost the speaker nothing, to be thrown away, as fickle fancy changes, or the gold, for which the words were spoken, is squandered in "riotous living." Oh! we must not speak too confidently of woman's equal strength with man. The *head* may be, and no doubt often is, fully equal, but there must be a *weak spot* in woman's *heart*, or we should not be so often deceived by those oily speeches, despairing glances, and vows of undying constancy, which have made so many of the best and noblest of our sex, the patient victims of man's arbitrary power. We must learn to distinguish the ring of the *true gold* from the "base alloy" (for, thank God, there are true, constant, loving hearts to be found among the *higher powers*); or, if deceived, prove that we have strength to cast the traitor from us forever, or consent to be called the "*weaker vessel.*"

As day dawned, a step outside alarmed Mrs. Herbert, and hastily closing the door, she passed from the room, dreading to meet the wretched being she had that night vowed to watch over, and seek to lead toward peace and heaven.

But it was good Dr. Strong, who, with an unusually excited manner, inquired—

"How is Mrs. Reed?"

"At rest!"

"Thank God she is spared one sorrow. Her husband has but now breathed his last, raving in *delirium tremens.* May I never witness such another deathbed. His face, foreshadowing the torments of the lost, is still before me, and I feel as if I could almost hear their 'weeping, wailing and gnashing of teeth.' And the kind-hearted physician shuddered.

"Then come with me," said Mrs. Herbert, "and I will show you such a contrast, that as you gaze you will imagine that you hear the angels, who, with songs, and everlasting symphonies, bear our departed mother safe to the 'happy land.'"

The next day was the Sabbath, and after giving

notice of the death of this mother in Israel, Mr. Herbert preached from Rev. xiv. 13: "Blessed are the dead who die in the Lord, from henceforth. Yea, saith the Spirit, that they may rest from their labors, and their works do follow them."

He spoke of the various answers one would receive, who should inquire among men, "Who are the blessed?

"With the Brahmins, it would be, he *who is annihilated.*

"With the Mohammedan, he *upon whom Houris wait.*

"With the Indian, he who reaches the *great hunting grounds, where success and victory are sure.*

"And even among civilized, Christian communities, there is a wide difference in men's opinions of the *meaning of true blessedness.*

"With one, *wealth* is the key by which to gain an entrance into the desired haven.

"Another feels that he could be truly blessed, if the eyes of an admiring world were to follow his efforts. That would be the height of *his* ambition.

"Another longs for Pleasure to enwreath his brow, and place her sparkling cup to his lips.

"But ask of God, who truly knows and sees all things from the beginning, and he replies:

"'Blessed are the *dead who die in the Lord.*'

"The righteous dead rest from temporal care and spiritual labor for Zion, and for sinners. They are no longer uncertain as to the grand issue of their probationary state. They at once and forever *rest* from sin, and the temptation to it.

"They are united to God. They see him as he is, are constantly in His presence, instructed by His lips, and led by Him through eternity in progressive steps of holiness and happiness.

"Their *example remains*, to win sinners and comfort saints. Their prayers, yet to be answered, their conversations and entreaties for children and friends, remain in God's hands long after they are gone, to be used by Him, for the conversion of those for whom they labored while on earth.

"Think of the friend who has now gone from us. Will her deep interest in the cause of religion in this church—her faith and trust in God—her meekness and humility—her charity to the faults of others, and her unwearied benevolence, ever be forgotten, by those of us who have been so pleasantly associated with her?

"Will not, then, her labors of love live after her, continually bringing forth, fruit which shall *follow* her to that blessedness upon which she has entered? There is hardly a roof under which she has not been found, on errands of mercy or kindness, by night and by day. I call upon you to notice the superiority of *goodness* over everything else in society. I think more persons of every class were wont to visit her humble residence, than any other in this place. And why?

"Was it for *wealth? She had none.*

"Was it for *flattery?* She always spoke *plainly*, and *always* spoke the *truth.*

"It was the loveliness of a true *Christian character* which drew all to her. She *has her reward*, and angels *now* love, *whom we loved.* We have sustained great loss, by that which was her unspeakable gain. Imitate her, dear friends, so far as she imitated Christ, and God give us all to meet her about his throne."

This is but a feeble outline of a sermon which was not soon forgotten.

CHAPTER VIII.

A WELCOME GUEST.

It is a soft, lovely night in June. The little village of Glenville sleeps as calmly, wrapped in its moonlight mantle, as though no sorrow could find its way into so peaceful a scene. But there is no rest in the pastor's abode. Anxious faces are around the bed. Pale as marble, Mr. Herbert tenderly wipes the drops of agony from the sufferer's brow, speaking words of hope, which his own heart scarcely believes, and the unconscious Mary does not recognize, as the terrible convulsion shakes her frame.

"Oh, mother! mother!" The first words she has uttered for hours, and the strong man bows his head upon her pillow, in anguish of spirit. What would he not give if that mother were only there to comfort and direct! Hours pass unheeded—but at length, hearts, well-nigh hopeless, were cheered by a favorable change. Consciousness returned, and as the sun rose over the town, bathing the green hills of Kentucky with floods of glory, little Susie Herbert opened her blue eyes upon a strange, new world, and her father's glad heart went forth in gratitude for the precious gift, and still more for the mother, spared to bless both father and child.

The first two weeks after the birth of the little one, were filled with uncommon suffering, increased, and in part caused, by the inexperience of the kind, but very unsafe nurse, who had volunteered to remain with Mrs. Herbert till she was once more able to take charge of her family herself.

Proud and happy in the new relation of *father*, George forgot his dislike to letter-writing, and communicated the tidings to the friends on both sides, in a series of amusing, and most graphic epistles. The *child* was a wonder. The *mother*, beyond all praise—but the *nurse*!— If I could but obtain the description of the good lady, as sent to Mrs. Leighton, it would stamp this little narrative with immortality forever.

At the end of three weeks, Mrs. Herbert concluded to try the experiment of resuming the labor for her family, fearing that if her good-natured, but very untidy attendant, remained longer, she should have a second edition of house-cleaning, worse than the first.

Taking advantage, therefore, of her husband's absence for a fortnight, she signified her intention of "*pitching into it*," as Miss Polly elegantly expressed it, and they parted the best of friends. Polly, perfectly satisfied that *Miss* Herbert never would have "picked up so cheery" had it not been for her successful nursing, and Mary, equally certain that nothing need ever annoy her after living through these three weeks.

Susie proved herself a jewel of a baby—a happy little pigeon, cooing or sleeping night and day—and her mother thought that she should find time and strength to have everything in order and homelike, before her husband's return. She had been moving about some time, and was beginning to feel that if "the spirit was willing, the flesh was weak," when good old Mother Morton came in to see her.

"Now that's just what I expected," said she. "I saw your woman pass with her bundle, and says I to Martha Ann, I'll run round to the minister's awhile, for I'm thinking Polly, good soul, has not left things as nice as she found them. *Miss*

Herbert will have hold of the scrub-brush before I get there, I'll venture, and that won't answer, no-how. You see now, honey, I'm eenmost as good at guessing as your Yankee folks, for here you are, all pale and trembling, and I'll warrant have done more than two women's work since she left. She's a good creature, and no one means better; but she ain't neat, it must be admitted, and may be she isn't to blame for that. We all have our gifts and graces, you know. But, dear soul, you just give here that cloth and brush now."

"No, no, dear Mother Morton, you must not do this. I have been working very slowly, and will stop now and talk with you."

With a loving smile, Mrs. Morton put her two stout arms about Mrs. H., and tenderly laid her on the bed, by the baby.

"There, keep still, and watch these little blue eyes. 'Tain't often that I meddle with other people's business, but I don't exactly feel that I am doing so now. You've left your mother and home, to come off here with Mr. Herbert to help do good, and 'twould be a shame if some of us old bodies didn't watch over you a little. Mother Reed thought 'heaps on you,' and with good cause, and there are others who maybe think as much."

"We haven't a great 'chance' of money, but we've got hands a deal stronger than your'n. Now see how soon I'll have some of Miss Polly's grease-spots out," and while her words flowed steadily on the brush, was not idle.

A noble-hearted woman was Mrs. Morton, and Mary knew and appreciated her worth, and understood also, that in no other way could she make her kind friend so happy, as to allow her to carry out the wishes of her benevolent heart. So she fondled her child a few moments, and then dropped gently to sleep by its side.

Mrs. Morton came and stood over the sleepers, silent and sadly, while the tears rolled freely down her furrowed cheek, and at length she passed softly into the next room.

"Poor thing!" she said to herself; "it makes me a child to see one so fair and delicate come to wear out and die here. She is full of courage, and not a bit proud; but preachers *is* poorly paid, and their wives work hard and break down soon in this climate. Somehow I wish I could just take that woman and her baby, and put her back into her mother's arms. But Mr. Herbert wouldn't thank me for that, and I'm sure we couldn't spare her ourselves. Well, the Lord will provide."

Mary woke quite rested and surprised to find that it was nearly noon. Mrs. Morton had done wonders toward obliterating the spots and stains of the last weeks, and was tying on her sun-bonnet, ready to leave.

"Why did you let me sleep so long, dear Mrs. Morton?"

"Why didn't you sleep *longer*?" said she, laughing. "Now just you keep quiet; or, if that's asking too much, take your sewing. I'm going to run home a minute, and then come back and invite myself to dinner. Martha Ann is going to spend the day with a cousin, and I've a nice little chicken, and a lot of green peas and some biscuit, I reckon about as good as your mother could give you. So I shall bring them over, and we'll eat them together."

Without waiting for thanks, she hurried away, and soon returning, began to prepare the table for their dinner.

"At least, let me help you now," said Mary.

"No, no. Keep quiet. I see you've been looking over bills and papers, and are sober and troubled. Don't let these things vex you. Money matters always do get into a snarl when a body is sick; but time and patience will cure all such things."

"Close economy, and no little hard work, must be added, to complete the cure, I imagine, my kind friend," said Mrs. Herbert, smiling, "and I am intending to call you in as my consulting physician."

"Well, well. Let's leave business alone till we've had our dinner, and perhaps that may put a little color into those pale cheeks, and give you more strength to arrange matters;" and soon a most inviting meal was placed on the neatly-laid table.

"If Mr. Herbert were only here, now, this would seem quite homelike. I feared some of the time Miss Polly was with us, that my good husband would famish; and yet, with all the discomforts of the past three weeks, *these bills* show that our expenses have been double that of any two months of our previous housekeeping."

"I can easily believe that. It's common talk, how nicely our minister and his wife contrive to live on almost nothing. How *do* you do it? And how did you manage, as unwell as you have been this winter, to do all your work yourself, till the very day baby was born?"

"Oh, it's because I have such a capable husband. He can make a bed, sweep, wash dishes, make coffee, cook a steak, and make better bread than half the housekeepers in the land.

"But now I want to consult you. We can never get along with as little as we have done. By taking in sewing all winter, I was enabled to lengthen many a short place, but with little puss—good as she is—I foresee I can do little beside our own sewing, and, indeed, I think sewing so steadily injures me."

"That I am sure it does. Dr. Strong says he only wonders it didn't kill you."

"Well, what do you think of my renting the whole of this house, and taking a few boarders? Mr. Dudley moves to-morrow into his new home, and has offered to let me have the whole of this tenement, for seventy-five dollars per year!"

"Why, that is not double what you pay for these two rooms alone, and it is four times as large. What does it mean?"

"Just this, I imagine, Mrs. Dudley has been a true friend ever since we have been here, and couldn't well help seeing that it was pretty close work to make our quarterly payments. I presume she has been using her influence with her husband for our benefit.

"Shall I accept the offer? I must decide to-day, for I know Mr. Dodge wants the house, and has offered a hundred dollars for it."

"If it were not for the hard work you will bring upon yourself, poor dear, I would say accept at once, for you'll never have so good an offer. But what will Mr. Herbert say?"

"He will be sorry for the necessity, of course, and perhaps, at first, be reluctant to admit that any such necessity exists; but he can't well fail to see it after looking over these papers," said Mary, laying her hand on the pile of bills. "And beside, if I get all nicely moved, and everything in order, with the boarders on hand, what *can* he do *but submit*, and be, for once, the dutiful husband he boasted himself to be, the last time you saw him."

"Well, you and Mr. Herbert beat all, for taking everything merrily. But let me tell you, if this thing must be done, you will allow the old woman to help you move, and in any other way she can. But you aint going to have any boarders till you are a '*sight*' stronger than you are now."

"Oh, yes; if I take the house I must make it '*pay*' at once; and my maxim is, the more people use their strength, the more they'll have."

"Well, I don't like it a bit; but if it must be, I can secure you four good boarders for next Monday; you shan't have them a day sooner. There are two ladies and two gentlemen—I wish I could find all gentlemen; for every housekeeper knows, their business calls them out so much, it is less trouble than boarding ladies; but these are all I know of now."

"Thank you, thank you! what a comfort you are to me! And will you add to your favors by telling me if there is any place, short of the city, where I can rent second-hand furniture with little expense. Of course, it must be simple. We have only the furnishing of these two rooms."

"I was wishing to speak of that, but feared it might seem too bold; now, however, I will tell you. Before my man died, we used to board our ''prentice boys;' but now there is no one but Martha Ann and myself; I have a '*heap* of *plunder dumped* down' in my garret. It's plain, but comfortable, something like what you have here. If you'll use it till I call for it, and make no words about it, I shall consider it as a favor."

Mrs. Herbert "made no words," but putting her arms round the kind lady's neck, kissed her most affectionately, and I doubt not, it was a more valuable return to her than money could have been.

The next day Mrs. Dudley moved out, and gave up the house to Mrs. Herbert. A few moments after the keys were handed her, Mrs. Morton walked in

"Well, here's the housin'-stuff; are you able to tell us where we are to place it?"

"Why, but dear Mrs. Morton, don't the rooms need cleaning, before putting anything into them?"

A hearty laugh was the reply.

"I know you are thinking—oh dear!—these Hoosiers don't understand how to do anything, neatly."

"Oh, no. There's no fear I should say that of you, at any rate, after having once seen your home. But I only thought it would be so much easier cleaning while the house was empty."

"Sartain; and Mrs. Dudley's had a woman at work with me all day, scouring each room as fast as her things were taken away; and 'tis all in order. I was 'despi't feared' you'd find it out, when we were at work in the room opposite."

Mrs. Herbert's thanks may be imagined, and also all the planning and contriving, between the two ladies, till their work was done, and *well done.*

The next morning, Mrs. Morton sent the gentlemen, and came soon after with the ladies, to make all arrangements requisite to their becoming members of the pastor's family. It was decided that they should make their appearance at dinner on Monday noon.

When this was settled, Mary felt that she had opened another volume in life's history, and longed for her husband's presence, that they might begin it together. A week elapsed before his return, and then, though he feared the burden would be too severe upon his wife, he could not fail to see a necessity for some increase of their means of support, and this, he hoped, would be less injurious than such constant application to her needle had been.

A year passed quickly by, bringing cares, labors, and anxieties to our friends, as to others, but far more of peace and true happiness, than all the luxuries wealth can give, or than generally falls to the lot of mortals.

Loving messages from Hill Farm were very frequent, and Mary's bright and hopeful replies were filled with amusing pictures of their home life, and glowing, mother-like descriptions of little Susie—the pet and plaything of all.

Meanwhile, Mr. Herbert's talents and efforts began to be more widely known and appreciated, and occasionally Glenville was thrown into a fever of excitement by rumors of "*calls*" received, or to be received, from some of the most important points in the State. The people of his charge were beginning to look upon him as *their own*, and felt it little less than robbery, to seek to take him from them. A lot had been bought, and plans were on foot to build a larger church, with a house near by for a parsonage. Other denominations had pledged assistance, and the pastor's salary was to be increased one hundred dollars, with the promise to make it still more liberal another year.

At this crisis, a pressing invitation was extended to Mr. Herbert, to remove to a neighboring city of considerable importance, and take charge of a new enterprise in that place. The invitation was at once rejected; again repeated, and a second time refused. A *third* application, still more urgent, was enforced by such strong arguments, for a more careful consideration of the matter, that he dared not dismiss the question without consulting his older brethren in the ministry.

How anxiously did the little church wait for that decision! Petitions were signed from all classes and all denominations. The parsonage was besieged with those who came entreating, with tears, that they would not forsake them, until both Mr. and Mrs. Herbert were half sick with the excitement.

The first Sabbath after the synodical consultation, Mr. Herbert was obliged to make their decision public. How many trembling hearts were assembled in the dear little church on that bright summer morning! The house was crowded, when the pastor and his wife entered, and one glance at their pale, sad faces was enough. A sob, almost a groan, passed through the congregation. The prayer and sermon was a most excellent preparation, for what, all knew, they must hear—replete with tenderness and love, making his people ready to cry out, "how can we give him up?" and yet convincing them that nothing but the sternest conviction of duty could have persuaded him to a separation.

After the sermon, Mr. Herbert announced his decision formally, and told them frankly the steps by which he had been led, and explained the reasons why his brethren felt that he ought not to hesitate.

They were such, and so strong, that even his sorrowing people could not gainsay them. He was to remain some weeks longer, and would do all in his power to supply them with another pastor before leaving.

About this time little Susie began to show symptoms of illness, from teething, and as the warm weather progressed, she failed rapidly.

For many days they watched her, scarcely able to perceive the feeble breath. Every arrangement had been completed for their departure to the new field of labor, but the darling of all hearts could not be moved, and the prospect was every hour more probable, that they would be obliged to lay her little form to rest among the people of their first home.

One morning, the physician announced a change, saying a few hours would decide, whether for life or death, and advised, if favorable, that they should commence their journey immediately, in a private carriage, as riding would be the best restorative for the child, if taken slowly.

At noon, Dr. Strong assured the anxious parents that by great care, and the most judicious nursing, their little one would recover.

The next day Mr. Herbert preached his parting sermon to a weeping congregation. We will not linger over this trying time, and the most affectionate farewells exchanged, as their loved teacher and friend passed from the little church for the last time.

It was sad for all, but most for the young pastor and his wife. Here had been their "wedded love's first home," and no other spot could ever have, for them, half its charms. They turn from well-known, true and faithful friends, to strange scenes, and untried hearts, not knowing what shall befall them there.

CHAPTER IX.

NORTON.

The journey was a delightful change, from the cares and anxieties of a sick-room, and the keen sufferings of parting from their people. Little Susie improved visibly with every hour, and her parents were soothed and comforted by the pleasant ride of four days. A kind friend had furnished them with an easy carriage and a good horse, and they were at liberty to travel so leisurely as to feel it restful, rather than fatiguing.

It was almost sunset when they came in sight of their future home. To our friends it bore little resemblance to all their past ideas of a city. It was more like one of the large flourishing towns of New England in size, but without the varied and beautiful scenery, which usually characterizes such towns.

They looked in vain for some bold feature in the

landscape. A hill, a bit of wood, or even a moss-grown rock, would have been a positive luxury.

"How I shall miss the river, and the bold Kentucky hills beyond!" said Mr. Herbert; "and the 'puff,' 'puff,' of the great boats, passing and repassing hourly!"

"Yes, we shall regret all these; but most I dread the vain longings for the old familiar faces. Good Doctor Strong, kind, simple-hearted Mother Morton—always ready in the hour of need. Poor Mrs. Gilbert, whom I had hoped to watch over and comfort, in her passage to the 'better land.' And dear Deacon Blake and wife, so prompt, yet so delicate and unobtrusive, in all their attentions—how can I leave them all, and form new ties among this strange people?"

"Is it harder, dearest, than to leave your old home, father, mother, and all, to go with me among those equally strange, yet who have now become so dear?"

"Ah! I know it seems very foolish, my dear husband. But I had then little experience, and saw everything in such a bright, hopeful light. We have passed through some dark, rough places since then, dear, and know that there are, most probably, still darker in the future; I shrink from meeting them here, whatever they may be."

Mary's tears were dropping silently over her sleeping child, and her husband at once divined the direction of her thoughts.

"Why, Mary dear, this is not like your usual hopefulness. I see you are 'borrowing trouble' for 'little puss' here. I, on the contrary, am greatly encouraged. How much she has improved in the last three days. When we started, I had little hope of bringing her thus far, alive, and now she is gaining hourly. Cheer up, darling, you must not show so sad a face when we greet our new people."

"This little pale, doll-like creature, in my arms, will be excuse enough for a sad face; but I will try and be cheerful for your sake, my husband."

"That's my own good wife. And now here we are, and there are Elder Jackson and his lady waiting at the gate. You can't help liking her, I know."

Our friends were most cordially welcomed, and the sweet-faced, beautiful woman who met Mary, with a kiss as warm as if she had known her for years, won her heart at once.

We will leave the history of "first impressions" to be gained from Mrs. Herbert's earliest letter to her mother.

"NORTON, *Aug.* 3, 18—.

"MY DEAREST MOTHER:

"My last letter told you of the 'call' to this place, and the pain it cost to decide that we ought to come, and also the added trial of our dear baby's illness. George wrote you the morning we left Glenville, that she was better, and that letter you have received, no doubt.

"We were four days on our way here. One of the elders of this church came for us with his horse and carriage, and learning how low little Susie was, left them for us to come on slowly, and returned himself by stage.

"The journey has greatly benefited her, but still, it hardly seems possible that she can recover. I never saw so sick a child. Why, my dear mother, she is fourteen months old, and weighs but a pound and a half more than she did the day of her birth. Before her illness she was an uncommonly large child. But the ladies here tell me that such changes from teething are very common in this climate, and seem to feel quite sure she will now gain rapidly. God grant it. But I fear I am weak in faith.

"We are staying for a few days with one of the principal men of the church, and find a very pleasant family and comfortable quarters. Mrs. Jackson is one of the most lovely women I ever met, and, if I may judge from so short an acquaintance, is as 'good as she is bonnie.' She has quite a large family (your number, I think), and yet does not look much older than I do.

"Her family seem to look to her as to all that is good and perfect in woman, and yet I think they are troubled and anxious about her. She strikes one as exceedingly delicate.

"The daughters are very pleasant, well-informed girls, far superior to any I have met with since I left home, but none of them will ever be as fair to look upon as their gentle mother.

"We are to take possession of a little cottage near by, next week, ready furnished, which we can have a few months perhaps, but hope by that time to be able to make some permanent arrangement.

"The people promise us a more liberal support than we had at Glenville, but I am a little fearful that the promises may not be so reliable as with the dear church we have left.

"*They* were, to be sure, able to do but little; but they invariably went *beyond* what they engaged to do. George is, as usual, sure it 'will all come out right.' He is ever more sanguine about matters *coming right* than I am; but the worst of it is, I am sorry to say, that in *money matters* my view of our affairs is generally the most correct. If the worst comes, however, we can take boarders again, though I have a great longing to live just in my own family, for a little while at least. We have so much visiting to do, that it seems almost a necessity that the *home*, 'however homely,' should be ours alone—a resting-place from all outside cares and turmoil.

"Have had many calls from our new friends, and find some that bid fair to prove pleasant acquaintances; but, thus far, I can't feel 'drawn to them,' as I was when I first met the people of Glenville. There is more *profession* of interest, but I doubt if I shall find as much *heart*—that kind of heart which one can rest securely upon, when the dark days come. Perhaps because I am older and more experienced (one learns fast in this country), and do not take people upon trust as readily as formerly; perhaps I am a little *cross and soured* by this parting, and my heart closes itself against the idea of receiving a *new love*, so soon after leaving *the old*. If that is the reason, I must not indulge it—and will not.

"When we received this call, we were informed by the people of Glenville that it was a place greatly subject to the fever and ague; but Norton folks assured us it was a false report—that it was an unusually healthy place. Still, as we drew nigh, on our journey hither, my heart misgave me. It is a broad, level stretch of land as far as the eye can reach, looking as if one good, thorough rain would transform it into an impassable morass. How the inhabitants contrive to get about in rainy weather I can't imagine, unless they use stilts. The city itself has been reclaimed in part from this slough, and presents quite a thriving appearance, being very prettily laid out, with a number of fine buildings. Excepting in the main business streets, the houses are not so *huddled* together, after the manner of our eastern cities; but each has a fine back and front yard, and the streets are broad, with shade-trees on either side. On the whole, when seen on a fair, sun-lighted day, it is rather attractive at first sight; but after a while the eye tires of the sameness, and longs for some one or two elevated points to rest upon, if it be but a mole-hill. The village on 'the Plains' near home will give you some idea of this place; only you must shut out all those high hills, and woods, and farms which encircle 'the Plains,' and give them their greatest charm.

"After tea, the evening we arrived, a little boy I had not seen, came into the parlor. He was in good flesh, but so pale and *blue*. 'Is he ill?' I asked the mother.

"'Oh, nothing but the chills.'

"'They must be very common, if you speak of them so calmly,' I replied.

"'Oh, yes,' said the eldest daughter, smiling; 'we *take turns* in having them. We should not feel *at home*, unless some one was *shaking* about the house. It's nothing so dreadful, Mrs. Herbert; everybody makes light of it—*after it is over*.'

"'Don't look so distressed, and gaze so sadly on your little one,' said Mrs. Jackson; 'chills are not the worst troubles in the world. To be sure, they are not very desirable, but fatal consequences, arising from them, are rare.'

"'But, Mrs. Jackson, we have been sadly deceived. We were informed, before we decided to come, that this region of country was subject to "fever and ague;" but the gentlemen from Norton, to whom my husband went to learn the truth of the report, assured him most earnestly that it was not so; and *on that assurance* we decided to come. They knew we should have declined had we known this; for lightly as you speak of this disease, we know that, in the end, it undermines the health and ruins the constitution, and we should have felt it a sin, voluntarily to place ourselves in such a position.'

"I could not help seeing the look of astonishment which passed round the little circle.

"'Are you sure,' said Mrs. Jackson, 'that there is not some mistake? I cannot understand what any one could expect to gain by giving you information, the falsity of which you could not fail to learn by a week's residence; and surely any one must see far enough ahead to realize that, once known, it would weaken your confidence in us as a people.

"'The whole region has always been noted for fever and ague, ever since it was settled. When

Mr. Jackson and myself first came here it was frightful; but as the country round about became drained and settled, it has gradually decreased, or rather become much less severe.'

"As I looked at the delicate face before me, and marked the hectic flush on her cheek, while she spoke, I could not but think that '*only the chills*,' though perhaps a slow death, might, nevertheless, prove a sure one.

"I fear I may have said too much and prejudiced them against me, at the beginning. But it was so trying to feel that I had brought my poor baby from so healthy a place as Glenville! Well, it is done, and fretting won't help the matter; I think I will not tell George of it, however; it will dishearten him, at a time when he needs all his courage, to learn that the people with whom we are to dwell, in order to accomplish their wishes, should so forget the truth.

"I wish I had not learned it myself—at least, till I had become more at home, and better acquainted with these new friends.

"I must close now; I fear you will be troubled with this letter, dear mother, and it might have been more generous had I waited till I felt in better humor, with all the world, and with this place in particular. I have acted on Cowper's principle, though I don't believe in it. He says, 'What's the use of having friends, if we don't let them bear a part of our burdens.'

"But I've no doubt I shall feel as happy as ever in a week. Why not? I have my husband and child safe as yet. Indeed I feel better satisfied already. You see, Harry dear, I'm giving you the benefit of enough '*bile*' to save me at least a year from the *shakes*. Isn't that good logic, father?

"And now good bye. When I am fairly *at home* once more I'll write again.

"Most lovingly,

"MARY HERBERT."

Mrs. Leighton's reply to this contained one piece of advice, which I insert for the benefit of all loving wives. After expressing great sympathy, and her fears for the health of her daughter and family, she adds:

"But, my dear Mary, I must reprove you a little. I notice in your letters to me, that frequently, after alluding to some little annoyance, or trial hard for you to bear, you say, 'I tell you, dear mother, of these petty grievances just to relieve my mind, but I never go to George with *my* troubles. I would not for the world hinder his usefulness, or take his mind from his labors by speaking of trials which I can bear alone.'

"Your intentions are excellent, my dear child, but I do not think you judge correctly. I believe it is for the happiness of husband and wife to be *one, so truly* that they shall share with each other all things, that even in the *smallest* matters there shall be the most perfect confidence and openness. The promise was '*for better or for worse, for joy or sorrow.*' It is, I think, a mistaken idea, that a clergyman's mind should be constantly shielded from all the little rubs and irritations of life, and especially that his wife ought to conceal all her anxieties and perplexities, and be ready, under all circumstances, to meet her husband with an unclouded brow which, when her heart is troubled, means, in plain English, that she ought to play the hypocrite, to save his feelings. Such a course is an insult to a husband's manliness of character, and will eventually spoil any man, unless he is already an angel. Now, I do not believe our dear George is quite angelic yet, but he is far too good and noble to be made vain and selfish by his wife's using herself as a shield to ward off little trials. *Great troubles any* man can bear, but your husband will grow in grace much faster, and go on unto perfection all the more easily, if he learns to meet petty vexations with equanimity; and you, my child, will live to aid him much longer, and far more effectually, if you 'bear one another's burdens,' instead of one little silly girl's attempting to carry the whole load for both. Try it, my darling; or, years hence, when you are growing old, perhaps feeble and incapable of such exertions as you now make, you will yearn for comfort and aid from him, and find, too late, that your husband has so well learned the lesson *you* have yourself taught him, that he cannot readily *unlearn* it, and if you *then* claim his sympathy and affectionate support, he may feel that you *are* encroaching on time devoted to the duties *of his high calling.* *Then* it will not do for you to remind him that there are other duties, equally binding as those which belong to his public life.

"But I have warned you, and will add no more."

"Poor mother!" said her daughter, after reading the letter. "The warning is tinged by the dark shadows of her own experience. But the 'lines have fallen unto me in pleasant places,' so far as my married state is concerned. In this matter there is, certainly, no cause for fear. My husband *couldn't* become selfish under any circumstances, and will not fail me in the hour of need, I know. So long as I am strong and well, I really think it is my duty to keep all care from him, that I can. Dearest mother! she can't exactly understand how I am situated. My lot has been so different from hers. Dear George! how often I long to have mother with us, that she may see for herself how good, and kind, and considerate he is to her silly daughter! If I could use my *mind* to any purpose as many wives can, it would change the aspect of things materially. But I, unfortunately, am only fit for simple, domestic duties, and can make mysel f*necessary* to his happiness, only *through little things.* I will never conceal anything from him that will increase his happiness, but I think I must not show him this letter; it would grieve him, I fear."

Ah, Mary! you are letting your *heart* and not

your *head*, guide you now; you have already learned to fear, as well as love (though it would be hard to make you realize it), not from a shadow of coldness or harshness on his part, but because you, foolishly, place too high an estimate on mental qualifications, and too low on good, plain common sense, and therefore fear that the *latter* will not prove sufficient to retain your hold upon his affections, unless you add to it the sacrifice of your ease and quiet, to guard him from annoyance. Some men would soon learn to *claim* it as a *right*, instead of receiving it as the purest token of deep and true affection.

Mrs. Herbert's next letter was written immediately after the receipt of her mother's; and first replying to the home epistle, she then adds:

"I have delayed this longer than I intended, and fear you may have been made anxious by it; but my reasons will prove an abundant excuse, I am certain.

"While I was writing the first part of this letter, little Agnes came into my room weeping bitterly, saying her mother wanted me, for little Charlie (a sweet boy about Susie's age), was very ill. I was greatly shocked. Not two hours before, he was sitting on my lap, having a grand frolic with my little darling. I hastened to the room and found the poor child in a '*chill*,' and the symptoms developed were such, that the family were greatly alarmed, and when the physician came, he evidently shared their anxiety.

"*Afternoon.*—I have just left little Charlie, by whose sick-bed I have been watching, while his sorrowful mother tried to rest a few moments. Dear little fellow! He does not appear half so ill as our baby did—indeed, she still *looks* the sickest of the two. But I am sore afraid of this disease. I can hardly tell why; but ever since I came West, I have had a strange dread of it. Every one laughs at me for it, and assures me that it is nothing to be alarmed at; that it seldom proves anything serious. It may be so, but George attended *four* funerals yesterday, and has three to-day, from *congestion, following a chill!* I had never seen a case till Charlie was attacked, and to me it is something very frightful.

"George has just come in to inform me that we can move at once into the little cottage I spoke of in my last. It is a week earlier than we had hoped to obtain it. Mrs. Jackson urges us to stay till morning, but the house is all ready, the family who own it have kindly left food and all the needful for to-morrow's breakfast, and we feel that we ought to relieve our afflicted friends from the slightest additional care, as soon as possible.

"I will lay this aside and finish after we move; our trunks are all ready, and in a half hour I shall be getting tea, *at home*, once more.

"*Thursday morning.*—Oh, mother! dear little Charlie is dead! I have just finished his little robe, and dressed the darling boy for the *grave!* Dear mother, there is something so frightful in that thought, when connected with a *babe!* I cannot bring myself to realize, but that one so dependent on maternal love, will be all the while *conscious* of the dreary loneliness of its last sad resting-place, and the thought always makes me turn sick with horror! I earnestly wish I could divest myself of this idea, and feel, as on the burial of adults, that God has taken the spirit back to his own loving care, and that 'tis only the casket in which He placed our jewel, when He loaned it to us, that is hid in the cold earth.

"We were sent for this morning, before breakfast, and found the loved child in convulsions.

Poor Mrs. Jackson! she is very calm, but the 'iron has entered her soul,' and she looks so frail, and spiritual, I can't but think she will soon follow her beloved child.

"I have become truly attached to this family, but as the house is full of their relations and older friends, I still feel too much a stranger to remain longer, as all is done that I can do. I have, therefore, returned home, to prepare tea for my husband, who is again at a funeral; and while I wait for him, dear mother, I will finish this long-delayed letter.

"I feel very sad and lonely. It is a still, sultry, August day—a 'fever breeder,' as the doctor said this morning. Little Susie has fallen asleep on the settee. The clock ticks sadly on the mantel, the flies crawl lazily over the window, with a ceaseless buzz, that makes me shiver. The shadows of the beautiful locust-trees look ghostly, as they fall athwart the grass, or flicker noiselessly in the sunlight, on the floor. How painfully still it is! How new to me to feel so listless and half melancholy! If I wasn't ashamed of it, I could easily imagine I was going to be sick.

"The quiet is so unearthly that it almost frightens one. But there comes George, just turning the corner, and the sight of his cheerful, loving face will put all these fancies to flight.

"The clock has already changed its dirge-like tick, to a lively tone—the flies buzz merrily now, and the locust shadows haven't a bit of a ghost about them, but are dancing like fairies on the 'charmed green,' and the magician who has wrought such wonderful changes is at the door, so good bye, my dear ones, and don't laugh at me for this foolish fit of the '*blues.*'

"Your own,

"MARY."

CHAPTER X.

SICKNESS.

Poor Mary's despondency was not all imagination, but the precursor of illness. Before morning, the *dreaded chills* had her in their power, and in a few hours her husband was made captive also.

Mrs. Campbell, a kind-hearted Methodist neighbor, took the little puny Susie to her own house, her parents at the time too ill to realize that they might never see her again.

Mr. Herbert was for some days alarmingly sick; but his wife, from the first, appeared utterly prostrated, without strength to rally.

Her baby's name she never mentioned; but it was very sad to listen to her entreaties to be carried into her husband's room, if but for *one look*. No word of complaint for the severe sufferings she was enduring was uttered—only the one thought, her husband was sick, and she could not watch by his side.

These were sharp trials for our young friends. They had entirely left out of their calculations the possibility, that days and nights of weariness and pain could pass, unsoothed by word or look from each other.

Mr. Herbert was able to visit his wife's bed-side at the end of ten days. What a change had passed over both. Weak as a child, his feeble limbs could scarcely support him across the room; and can that pale, hollow-eyed woman be his blooming Mary?

Mr. Herbert gained rapidly, as most are expected to do after the "ague," but there were many causes to retard his wife's recovery. As she lost anxiety for her husband, she began to long exceedingly for the poor little one, who had been so unceremoniously made over to the care of others. She accused herself of heartlessness, because she had so easily yielded her to one whom she had never seen till the day she was taken ill.

The people of all classes showed much deeper sympathy than Mary's first impression led her to expect. One beautiful morning, when she had been ill about four weeks, a gentleman, whom Mr. Herbert had seen but once (and who took occasion to boast during the interview, that though Yankee born and bred, he hadn't been inside of a church for the last twenty years), rode up to the gate with a fine easy carriage, and a noble span of bays, and calling Mr. Herbert out, said smiling:

"I have come to give you and Mrs. Herbert a ride, if you will risk your neck with such a heathen driver. You see, I've a notion that Mrs. Herbert will recover more rapidly if she can see her baby. Dr. Marvel says it is a first-rate idea, and the ride will not hurt her at all.

"Many thanks, Mr. Upton, but Mrs. H. has not set up ten minutes yet, and cannot walk as many steps. I do not think I could possibly get her from her bed to your carriage."

"Have you lived in New England all your boyhood days, without learning how to make 'a chair,' to carry your sisters and playmates over the snow-drifts?" said Mr. Upton, laughing. "I did not suppose *you* were strong enough yet, to bring the lady here; but step in and help her up, and then we'll see if you and I together cannot take her to the carriage, as gently as you would carry your baby."

"You are exceedingly kind."

"Oh, nonsense. Don't talk of that, man; I've lived so long among these *confounded chills*, that I've a soft spot in my heart for all new-comers who take the ague; and—well—it may as well out—to tell the truth, sir, I'm a little ashamed of myself, for my rascally attempt at browbeating at our last meeting, and also for using rather '*tall*' language to you. If you had tried to *preach* to me just then, I reckon the spirit *to-day* would have moved me to turn my horses' heads in an entirely different direction; for, as you have seen, I'm not a great lover of preaching anyhow, and I certainly can't abide it out of the pulpit. There, *that job's over*, and now let's have the sick one ready."

With very little fatigue, Mary was removed from the bed to the carriage; and none but those who have lingered long in the dismal confinement of a sick room, can fully appreciate the privilege of breathing once more the pure, sweet air and the hope of returning health. With equal gentleness and care, her kind attendants conveyed her into Mrs. Campbell's tidy sitting-room, and then Mr. Upton went in search of the mistress of the family, and little Susie.

A cradle stood near the lounge, and in it a sweet

babe lay sleeping. Mr. Herbert rose, and bent lovingly over it.

"How kind of Mrs. Campbell to take charge of our feeble baby, when she had one of her own so near the same age."

"Yes," said Mary, "she is a noble woman. If we could only see our darling half as healthy, it would be such a comfort."

Just then the baby woke, and seeing only strange faces, began to cry, and Mrs. Campbell entered at the same moment. After welcoming her guests, she took the child, who clung half frightened to her neck, slily watching the intruders.

"Don't think me impatient, dear Mrs. C.," said Mary, "but I am anxious to see my baby."

"Then you will not acknowledge this little partridge? Forgive me, I ought not to tease you when you are so weak; do you not recognize little Susie?"

"Surely you do not mean to say that this stout, ruddy little girl is our own!"

"Certainly. I am surprised that you think her so changed. It has been so gradual that I did not once imagine you would not know her instantly; and waited longer than was consistent with good manners, that your first meeting might be without witnesses."

"Why, Mrs. Campbell, I cannot credit it. I do not see a shadow of resemblance. Even her eyes and hair have changed. *Come to mother, darling!* Why, George, she doesn't know us—her own *father and mother!*" And kind Mrs. Campbell did not think her ungrateful, when she hid her face in the pillows to conceal the tears.

"'Tis rather hard, it must be confessed; but I cannot wonder at her shyness, for you are both far more changed than the baby. And beside," added she playfully, "she but followed your example in her forgetfulness. The parents did not know the child—remember."

It was not long before Mr. Herbert had succeeded in coaxing the little one from its foster mother's arms, and was enjoying a grand frolic, somewhat after the fashion of the old times. Soon, one of Mrs. Campbell's pretty daughters brought in a fragrant cup of tea, and some very tempting viands, of which they partook with more cheerfulness and appetite than they had enjoyed for many days. To leave their little one was now all the harder, from having learned how readily a child may forget its home and friends, and when Mr. Upton called for them, he found the mother earnestly urging the propriety of taking her home. Mrs. Campbell would not hear a word of this, and Mrs. Herbert reluctantly agreed that it was not yet safe.

"Beside," said Mr. Upton, in his quaint manner, "I only bargained to drive the parson and his wife. Couldn't possibly take any more load. 'A merciful man is merciful to his beast.' There's scripture for you, Mr. Herbert. You see I haven't forgotten all my New England education, even if I am such a sad fellow as you had good reason for thinking the other day."

When they left Mrs. Campbell, it was settled that she should bring the dear baby home in a few days, and also a nice little German girl she had been training to take charge of her, and then, if Mrs. Herbert was still improving, she would leave them both.

In due time, the pet child and her tidy little maid returned, but the poor mother gained slowly, having slight chills every day, and often a week of very severe ones. Mr. Herbert meanwhile began to feel that he was strong enough to resume his pulpit labors. He made the attempt, and closed the afternoon service in a violent chill. Another sick week was the consequence, though slight compared with the first. And so the winter passed, preaching two or three Sabbaths, and then laid by for as many more.

During one of these attacks, the owners of the cottage returned, and much sooner than was expected. Of course our friends found it necessary to seek another tenement immediately. A small house was secured, exceedingly out of repair, and in a very uncomfortable neighborhood. The least possible amount of furniture was provided, and for that little they were compelled to involve themselves in debt, not large to be sure, but sufficient to cause them anxiety, although assured by the people, that as soon as the church should become a little settled, there would be no embarrassment concerning money matters.

Their new habitation proved so leaky and damp, that Mr. and Mrs. Herbert were, in two weeks after moving, again confined to their room. The chills returned with great violence, and as the owner of the house refused to make any repairs, they were, after three weeks' trial, compelled to vacate, and seek another residence, or die. With many failures and delays, they at length secured a comfortable little cottage, with a pleasant garden, and found themselves settled, by mid winter, with encouraging prospects of remaining stationary, at least for the year.

Mrs. Herbert, however, continued quite feeble, and being compelled to perform a degree of labor far beyond her strength, her recovery to the enjoyment of anything like comfortable health was very doubtful.

They could not procure a servant, for they had not the means; and having learned by this time that fair words and soft speeches could not clothe the naked or feed the hungry, they were again compelled to secure boarders to supply themselves with the necessaries of life; and, feeble and worn with repeated illness, this was far more reluctantly resorted to than when at Glenville. There, all was done for them that their people were able to do, and in many cases even more; and the closest economy and incessant toil were easier borne, because absolutely necessary. In Norton there was no such necessity.

There was wealth in abundance among their new people. The money wasted on parties and frivolous amusements every few weeks, would have comfortably supported their pastor's family a year, and given his wife an opportunity to rest and regain her strength.

Yet the church at Norton loved them, there could be no doubt of that; but they had not been taught to feel that a minister's labors were worth paying for. Is it not surprising that there should be in the world good, kind, sensible people, who, after a man has given labor and money freely, for many years of his life, to prepare himself for their service, are content that he should come among them, and devote time, talents, and his whole heart to them, yet feel that every farthing they dole out for his support, is something to be proud of—an *act of charity?* If they employed a physician, or a lawyer, would they, instead of a fee, make them a present of some trifle, and go away pluming themselves on their generosity? Why should medical and legal service be more highly appreciated than the patient labors of a minister of the Gospel?

CHAPTER XI.

ADVICE GIVING.

"The winter was over and gone, the birds whistled sweet on the spray," the lawn was decked in its robe of purest green, the warm spring sun was whispering lovingly to the little leaves to wake and come forth from their winter homes, and the early flowers were just showing their pretty buds, when a darling son was added to the heart treasures in the pastor's abode. But the mother, enfeebled by the obstinate chills and great over-exertion of the past year, lay many weeks, hovering between life and death; and just as she began to resume her usual life of care and labor, the baby returned to God who gave it. Trials had multiplied around their path steadily; but though, for a moment, cast down and disheartened, they had met and overcome them by patience and cheerful courage. But this was the first of life's darker shadows—one of those which sink into the depths of the heart, and though hidden from all eyes, nor time, nor change, nor prosperity even, can ever dispel. Bitterly did Mary mourn for her baby boy, and Mr. Herbert also felt the loss most deeply. But poverty cannot indulge in the luxury of grief, and heart-sorrows must not stand in the way of duties and labors which a pastor *owes* his people. The relation of minister and people is generally viewed as a sort of *one-sided* obligation. The *labor* is exacted to the uttermost farthing—the *pay* is of less consequence, and may wait a more convenient season.

And poor Mary must force back the tears, reserving that luxury for the lonely night's watches, and struggle up again, as best she can, to household labors and anxieties. And very heavy were these burdens for her feeble strength. None may realize them, save those who have passed through the deep and troubled waters of a western missionary's life. Her work must be done and well done, and always prompt, or she would lose her boarders; and if forced to resign that mode of adding to their support, what could she do? Certainly not resort to her needle again. What could she accomplish with that in her present health? She could more easily drag her aching limbs or shivering frame about the house, than attempt to "stitch, stitch, stitch, seam, gusset and band," with her blue, chilled fingers—for scarce a day now passed without a chill.

It was irritating to her over-taxed nerves, and yet a source of merriment sometimes to herself and husband, to listen to the curious and contradictory advice which was daily volunteered, as to the management of their private affairs. Gratuitous advice is, I believe, a part of every clergyman's experience; but it is not often of the same character as that which our friends received.

Mrs. Tompkins, a near neighbor, was sure Mrs. Herbert could get along with less expense, if she "would only hear to reason, and not be so 'set' in her own way."

One day the good dame told her husband, she felt it her duty to go over and have a right motherly talk with the Dominie's wife; and as *such* "duties" are in no danger of being neglected, not many hours elapsed before she had waited upon herself into the kitchen, where Mary was at work, remarking that she always "allowed" to make herself at home wherever she went, and "liked to see people in the 'thick' of their work."

Mrs. Herbert must of course leave her bread half kneaded, and sit down with her guest, who assured her she wasn't going to stay "but a minute," just for a word.

"You are a young woman," said she, "and I *felt like* it would be neighborly to step in and give you a little advice. You can't be expected to be as *cute* in managing as *them as is* older and had a *heap* of experience.

"Now, you see, it's sheer folly to expect to make anything by keeping boarders, with your *genteel notions.* Just you listen to me, now. Turn them adrift—get along with two rooms, and under-rent the rest of the house; that'll be so much saved, don't you see? Why, Tompkins and I never had but *one* room for six years after we were married, and had three children to care for. And then, *you* are too 'sit and high-going' in your ideas of house-keeping. You think you must have three meals a-day, and the table regularly set each time, and I *seed* as I passed through your dining-room a *table-cloth on, for all the world as if you were expecting company*—have to, I s'pose, if you keep boarders, and pies or puddings, I'll warrant, every day for dinner.

"Well, now I'll tell you: 'fore Tompkins made his money we got into the way of *arly* rising—for we had to *scratch proper hard, I tell you.* But the children, poor dears, don't like to get up o' mornings; and, says I to Tompkins, 'let them sleep, and take their ease while they are young. Long's their *pap's* rich, what's the use o' having them up?' Well, as I was saying, Tompkins and I get up still pretty early (no need for it now, only 'tis habit, I s'pose), we have our breakfast—a cup of coffee, bread and butter, and a bit of cold meat, does well enough for us—(s'pose from what I hear, *you* have all sorts of warm *fixings*). *We* take our meals in the kitchen, on the pine table and without a cloth, when we have no company, and our kitchen ain't half as nice as your'n. You see, when we built, I told Tompkins to fix up anything, cheap, for the kitchen and rooms for help, and put more money into the fancy part of the house. Not but what we could afford to have *all* parts fine; *but what's the use?*

"Well, as I was saying, we just have the coffee on the stove and the table standing, and when the hired man and girl get through their milking, they help themselves, and the young folks come down, one after another, justs as it suit them. Now, don't interrupt; just let me talk, and tell you all about it. Half the time we don't have a regular dinner. If we get hungry, nothing easier, you know, than to go to the cupboard and help ourselves. A cup of tea and some meat for supper is all *we do.*

"When we have company, why, that's another thing. I reckon then on a grand *blow out*, and get out my silver, and china (Tompkins paid one hundred and twenty dollars for that set, in New York), and damask table-cloths, and we all turn in and cook everything nice, that we can hear or think of, and when *'tis over* we take a week or two's *resting spell.*

"Now *you* needn't have company; 'tisn't expected of a preacher's family; excepting a country parson, now and then, or travelling agent, or delegate, or such like" (which generally means having an extra plate about every other meal, thought Mary), "and if you'd just do *like* we do, when alone, you needn't work half so hard, and it wouldn't cost so much, by two hundred dollars a year, to support you; and *then*, you see, the church is young—hardly on its feet yet, and by being *saving*, you could relinquish at least that much of your salary and live on the rest."

Mary had been listening impatiently to this *long* lecture, and occasionally casting an anxious eye to the clock, thinking if the call was extended much longer she should be obliged to hurry beyond her strength, to have dinner in season, and as the good lady paused for lack of breath, she rose, saying,

"You must excuse me, at least for a time, Mrs. Tompkins; my bread will spoil, and my dinner be late."

"Well, but promise me you will do as I advise. Come, now, I must have *your promise*, so that I can tell my man, when he comes in, that you won't want *them two hundred dollars*. It's a promise, ain't it?"

"No, Mrs. Tompkins," said Mary, who had borne till patience was no longer a virtue. "No, indeed! It is to save something for the church, instead of relieving me from hard labor, and my husband from anxiety, it seems, about which you are so anxious. Why, madam, the church has been largely in our debt ever since we came, and has never paid up the full amount promised, nor anything, without constant solicitation. I *cannot* make the promise you require. The money we *must* have, or leave—*or die,* Mrs. T. And as for arranging household affairs after your pattern, you must excuse me. *I could not do it.* It may be the best and most comfortable way for you, but for myself and husband it would be intolerable. It wouldn't be living. I trust you will not be offended if I speak plainly; but indeed, madam, I cannot but feel that each one should manage their private affairs according to their own ideas of right, without interference, otherwise there can be no *home;* and I see no reason why a clergyman's family should not have that privilege, as well as others."

"Beg pardon! beg pardon! I might have known that a 'Yankee' would be too self-important to take advice from any one. Good morning. Interference indeed! I shan't interfere with *your* affairs again in a hurry, I can tell you," and she flounced out of the room in great wrath.

Poor Mary! Her head reeled, and her eyes were throbbing. She feared she had been too impatient, and longed to sit down and find relief in a hearty cry. But that would not do. The bread would be sour and the dinner late, if she yielded to any such folly.

"How could she be so cruel?" said she, half aloud, and little Susie opened her great, blue eyes, and shook her wise little head, saying:

"Susie tell papa; naughty *Topsins* scold poor mamma."

Mr. Tompkins began the world with a "fip" (Hoosier for sixpence), in Pennsylvania, and *speculated* with that, till he had the wherewithal to take him out "West" to a river town, and set up a cigar stall. He prospered, and took to himself a wife—a poor, uneducated, but industrious girl. He then built a log cabin, with only one room, as Mrs. Tompkins has said. While *he* traded cigars and candies, *she* washed for the boatmen who stopped near, or carded, spun and wove for the neighboring farmers. They lived in the rudest manner,—everything they touched turned to money, and was carefully invested in petty speculations.

In six years he moved to Norton, with property that warranted his going into business on a larger scale, and now, after a residence of over twenty years, he had built the finest house in the city, and furnished it to correspond. *That* was all for *show*. When by themselves, they lived just as his wife had described. And this woman's husband was worth half a million, yet felt that their pastor ought to give up two hundred dollars of his scanty support, to save his people the necessity of contributing *so liberally!* O selfishness! thou art hydra-headed, but hopelessly blind.

When papa returned, "Susie" made her threatened complaint of "Topsins," in the hearing of the young gentlemen, before her mother could check her.

"What is it?" said Mr. Herbert; "I don't quite understand the child. I wonder if you have been receiving a lecture as well as myself. Don't look so inquisitive. I shan't relate my experience, my dear, till I've had the benefit of yours."

Mrs. Herbert gave a concise explanation of the morning's trial, to the amusement, as well as indignation of her auditors.

"And so we are to be shipped," said young Burgess.

"*Possession* is nine points of the law," replied Stanly, "and I, for one, think I shall resist, if you attempt to serve a writ of ejectment against me."

"But, Mr. Herbert, pray let's have your adventures. I presume 'Pap' Tompkins has been giving you the counterpart of his wife's lecture."

"Yes, very nearly. Only he thinks because my wife is pretty, I am rather too easily influenced, and yield to her *fine notions* too readily—I don't govern her with real apostolic strictness it seems. So, my lady, you may look for vigorous discipline after this."

"That's too rich," said Townly. *He* dare not move without Mrs. Tompkins' consent. It is notorious. He might have sat for the portrait of Caudle."

"Oh, of course; but that's no reason why he shouldn't treat himself to a few independent airs, when out of her sight, poor fellow! Why, young gentlemen, if you were to hear some of my high-sounding, brave speeches when away from home, you would almost believe *I* was master of my own household. I cheat myself into that belief quite often.

"But do you know, wife, I'm going to dig up all your silly flowers in the front yard, and plant potatoes and cabbages instead. *You* entice me into spending a great deal of precious time over them, which I am *paid to devote to the interest of the church!*"

"The heathen!" said Burgess. "What did you say?"

"I trust you were more prudent and better natured than I was," said Mrs. Herbert.

"Not I, believe me. I gave him the benefit of my thoughts, without stopping to choose my words, and trust, if he repeats the conversation, it will warn others to let our private affairs alone for the future."

Weeks went by, and neither Mr. nor Mrs. Tompkins spoke to them, after this conversation, and if they saw them in the street, were careful to give them a *wide berth*, and a total alienation was fully expected.

One night, some weeks after, our friends were roused from sleep by Dr. Marvel, who requested Mrs. Herbert to hasten over to Mr. Tompkins', at once, as one of their daughters was very ill.

She found the house all confusion—Mrs. Tompkins in hysterics, and utterly incapacitated for any exertion, and though there were many neighbors and friends present, as was the custom in cases of extreme or sudden illness, they were more inclined to make pious reflections and sympathetic remarks, than to act efficiently or calmly.

Mr. Tompkins alone was self-possessed and able to assist; but there was such speechless, hopeless anguish in every line of his face, that it was more distressing than violent grief.

For two days and nights Mrs. Herbert never left that sorrowful abode, trusting her little girl and household cares with her husband, the sympathizing boarders, and a young friend who volunteered to remain with little Susie, when her father was obliged to join his wife in care for the afflicted ones, or was engaged in other and important duties.

The morning of the third day the sufferer was released, and even when the last sad offices were rendered, the mourners clung to Mrs. Herbert, beseeching her to remain; but she was exhausted, and obliged to return home. This severe tax on her strength confined her to her bed several weeks with a serious illness. Her kind attention in their deep afflictions, and her sufferings following, were never forgotten by the Tompkins family. Many a nice bit found its way to the "Dominie's" during her sickness, and any one who complained of

Mr. Herbert, or found fault with his wife, from that time forward, were sure to receive a more formidable lecture than those we have recorded. They could not do wrong, and it was no transient, impulsive feeling, manifested during the freshness of their grief, but an enduring affection, flowing out toward those who had served them in their hour of darkness—quiet, but most effectual in its developments.

When Mrs. Herbert began to sit up, Grandpa Tompkins, as he had taught Susie to call him, hovered about her sick-room, as patient and gentle as a woman, grudging any service or care that he could not render himself. It was amusing to see the earnest, and often laughable manifestations of the old man's solicitude and affection, and his wife's now gentle and unobtrusive kindness.

One morning, soon after breakfast, *Mr. Herbert* was *washing the dishes*, and his wife, sitting, pale and trembling, trying to wipe them, when, from the window, they saw Mr. and Mrs. Tompkins crossing the lawn. Their visits had been very frequent of late, and always the harbinger of some genuine kindness, but it was seldom that both came together, or so early in the morning.

"Our good friends have some great plan on foot, I'm sure," said Mr. Herbert, judging by their earnest, conscious looks.

"Well, we may be certain *now*," replied Mary, "that it will be something kind."

Their look of amazement, when they saw Mr. Herbert's occupation, was so irresistibly comic, that he dropped his dish-towel and laughed heartily. Mrs. Tompkins joined him, exclaiming, "Well, *now, did I ever!*" But Mr. Tompkins stood for a moment perfectly amazed, rolling his quid over and over in his mouth. Then thrusting his tongue into his cheek, with a peculiar knowing wink to his wife, he marched sturdily up to Mary, and wrapping the shawl around her, picked her up, chair and all, as if she had been a mere doll, and walked straight across to his own house.

"Stop, thief! stop, thief!" cried Mr. Herbert, as he and Mrs. Tompkins, with Susie in her arms, followed, as well as they could for laughing; and the boarders, who had devoted a part of the mornings, during Mrs. Herbert's illness, to assisting in the garden, dropped their tools and joined in the frolic.

In much less time than it has taken to write this

little incident, the bewildered invalid was safely landed in the pleasant parlor, and when the merry followers joined them there, Mr. Tompkins stood rubbing his hands with evident satisfaction and self-congratulation.

"There now, wife, I say that's a better way than to have tried *argufying* with the Dominie, and perhaps been worsted after all. Anyhow, Mr. Herbert, if you don't like it, you can just take the chair and your wife, and carry them back again. You'll find it something of a lift, though, I'm thinking."

"I shan't try it, you may be sure, sir. But what does this all mean? Are you in the habit of entering your neighbor's houses, and walking off with their wives in this style?"

"Not exactly. But, you see, I couldn't stand seeing that woman at work, and she so pale and shaky."

"Why," said Mrs. Tompkins, "we got Dr. Marvel's consent, and came this beautiful morning to invite you to spend the day with us, boarders and all; and see if a change wouldn't do your wife good; but when we saw what you were at, everything went out of my head but laughing; and if my man, here, hadn't started for home the way he did, I don't know as I should have remembered what I came for."

"It's a capital idea," said Stanly.

"Yes, and capitally *carried out*," rejoined Burgess. "And now *Mr. Herbert* may as well finish his dishes, and we *boys* will return and put the last touch to that weedy patch, and then go to our work."

"*You* can do just as you please, gentlemen; but Mr. Herbert must go with Tompkins, to see some sick folks, and I'll see that the women's work is cared for."

"Mrs. Herbert found the freedom and rest from care delightful; but said she should feel more natural if she had some little piece of sewing, to busy herself with, and requested that her work-basket might be sent for. But Agnes Tompkins stepped to the table, and handing her a bundle, said—

"Mother thought you'd never be easy without something in your hands, and therefore sent me to the store for this, last night; Sister Essie and I are to help make them."

On opening the bundle, there was material for four pretty summer dresses, and white linen for aprons for Susie, which were soon prepared by the willing hands of the young ladies.

Mrs. Herbert noticed through the day that every little while Mrs. Tompkins, or one of her daughters, would disappear for a few moments, and on returning, some significant glance passed between them, but nothing was said.

Toward night, the invalid returned home. Mary insisting that she could walk the few steps across the way, aided by her husband, while Mr. Tompkins followed with the chair, and his wife with Susie.

The mystery was then explained. Their kind friend had taken the house-cleaning into her own hands, and it had been thoroughly finished from top to bottom, and she priding herself on being able to prove to Mr. Herbert's satisfaction that he could not complain of his books or papers being confused or misplaced. They then bade each other good night, Mrs. Tompkins stopping, as she said, "just for a last word," to advise Mr. Herbert to examine the closets and pantries, and see if there was anything *missing.*

The tone with which this was said convinced them that there was something more than sport in the advice, and George concluded to follow it.

But in a moment he was back, insisting upon drawing his wife's chair into the store closet, that she might join in the examination. Oh! how easy a thing it is for true friendship to lighten heavy-laden hearts, and cause them to sing for joy!

There was flour, sugar, tea, coffee, rolls of nice butter, a ham ready cooked, and several uncooked; loaves of bread, still warm, cake and pies in profusion.

"Look!" said Mary, "there are two pans of milk that must have just been strained, for see, the foam is still on them."

A gentle, contented "low" near the window where she sat, caused them both to start, and raise the curtain, and there, tied to a stake, close by, stood a beautiful brindle cow.

"Oh, husband, I was saying at the table this evening, while partaking of that delicious cream, at our good friend's tea-table, what a luxury I should esteem it, could we afford to keep a cow—and here it is."

Could their friends have seen them as they stood in that little closet, among the gifts so unexpectedly showered upon them, they would have been abundantly paid for all their efforts.

"I will help you back to your room, dear wife and then I must run over and say one word, or shan't sleep to-night."

But, once in the midst of those who had been so thoughtful, *the words would not come.* He could only, with glistening eyes, shake each one affectionately by the hand, and look his thanks, and that was even more expressive than words could have been.

"There, now, we know just what you want to say ('tis the *first* time though, I ever saw you at a loss for words), Mr. Herbert. You see, my woman and I have never felt happy since we tried to '*gough*' you out of *them* two hundred dollars. We'd acted like better Christians, I reckon, if we had *added two more.*

"My boys and I have done the happiest day's work of all our lives, picking up those little articles, and *the woman* and girls have been even with us. If they can make your good lady's mind easier, till she gets strong, we shall be twice glad. I wish I could open other people's eyes to the worth of preaching, and the value of a good pastor, as fully as ours have been; but not *as ours* were opened—oh, no! If they will only wake up now, perhaps they'll escape learning the lesson as painfully as we have."

"But the cow, my dear sir—*the cow.*"

"She was our Annie's" brindle, said the old man, sobbing; "one that she petted, and loved ever since it was a week old. The morning after we lost our darling, it almost broke my heart to hear 'brindle' lowing about, and rubbing her head on my shoulder, as if she wanted to ask why her mistress had neglected her, and I vowed then, that Mrs. Herbert should have her. I only waited till she would be of service, to send her over, and the milk on your shelves is her first. My boys will take her to the pasture and bring her home with ours.

"Now, run off and look to *our* child, for such we shall always claim her, if she will let us. Tell her not to hurt herself being grateful—we are the debtors, and always shall be."

I trust our readers are not wearied with this sketch of Mr. Tompkins' family. Such as they were now, they ever remained, always watching to do good, to save their pastor from trouble, and many times Mr. Herbert must have been compelled to relinquish his charge, if it had not been for some timely aid from those friends, who always seem to know instinctively, when to come to the rescue.

CHAPTER XII.

A CHAPTER ON "HELP."

DURING the past year, Mrs. Herbert had occasionally been compelled by ill-health to hire a servant—or, as they were called, "*help*"—and her experience was, in many instances, of the most serio-comical kind.

At this period, there were but three classes of servants to be obtained—the Hoosier, German, and runaway, or free colored persons.

The Hoosier girls, who could be persuaded to "work out," were slatternly, uninformed and indolent, and withal so conscious of living in a *free country* (thousands of slaves almost in their sight, notwithstanding), that all the work they did was felt to be a condescension on their part, which demanded from their employers the largest amount of gratitude, and, at the same time, the highest wages. After remaining long enough in "a place" to receive the means of purchasing a new "*gound*," a bonnet, a bit of ribbon, and a few yards of lace, they would leave without a moment's warning, and stay idly at home, or sporting their finery among their neighbors, until the dress was bedraggled and torn, and the bonnet too shabby for further display, and then they were again ready to inflict themselves upon some poor, sick woman, who *must* have a few hours' service, even at the price of so undesirable an inmate.

The Dutch population were, generally speaking, exceedingly dirty, ignorant, and supremely selfish, —unmoved by kindness or compassion, thinking only for the "silver," and taking good care to get as much of that as possible, for the least amount of labor.

The colored people were mostly a lazy, good-natured race, content if they could bask in the sunshine, or sit over a large fire in the kitchen—knowing just enough of freedom to be unwilling to submit to dictation or control.

Mrs. Herbert had never been able to afford steady help, only a few weeks at a time, when incapacitated entirely for labor; and for that reason, she may have had specimens of more amusing or singular character, than she would have done, if employing constant assistance. Still her history in that regard, was but a fair average of the experience of the community generally.

Her first girl was a pretty, rosy-cheeked German, much more amiable and unselfish than most of her people; but exceedingly careless and unteachable. Always attempting the very things she was not expected or desired to do, and leaving undone those which belonged to her appropriate work, and of course making continually the most unfortunate and trying mistakes.

For instance, Mrs. Herbert was one day preparing to bake. Her pastry was all ready, and her bread light and sweet, in just the right condition for the oven, when she was interrupted by one of those friends, whose errand of life seems to be to assist patience to perform her perfect work, by making interminable calls on the busiest days of the week, and at the most unfortunate moment.

With a sigh, she washed her hands, took off her neat check apron, and prepared to entertain her guest, telling Maggie to finish slicing the apples, and then iron till she returned.

The lady's call was unusually protracted, and

poor Mrs. Herbert had before her eyes visions of a late dinner, and no desert, which, while she was liberally paid by her boarders, she felt it necessary to supply, especially as the customs of the place made a generous table all-important.

After a call of more than an hour, the lady rose, regretting that she could not spare time for a *longer tarry*, and took her leave.

The anxious housekeeper hastened to the kitchen, where Maggie met her with the broadest of smiles.

"The madam needn't hurry, and get into a '*boggle*' about dinner. I've made the pies, and have them in the oven, and see, the bread is doing nicely."

The kind intention was too manifest not to be met with thanks, though the matron's heart misgave her; for, from some specimens of her handmaiden's cooking, she could not hope her pies or bread would be of the best quality. On examination, however, the bread seemed right, and was "coming up like a puff," as Maggie said, and the pies when baked were tolerably fair to look upon.

So, comforting herself with the thought, that at

any rate it was too late to help it now, she hastened to finish other arrangements for dinner; and by the time the family were seated at the table, had regained a very comfortable state of mind.

The dinner passed pleasantly through the first course; but when the pies were set before her, a feeling of doubt again disturbed her, for she imagined that an unusual flavor was arising from them. But "too late to help it," again came to her aid, and passing a piece to each, she raised her eyes to judge of Maggie's success.

One bit had been tasted, and the plate put aside. Stanly sat with the expression of the most ludicrous indifference. Townly and Burgess had made trial, and with one quick glance at Mrs. Herbert, their attention was suddenly attracted to some apparent mystery in the figure of the tablecloth.

Mr. Herbert was a moment behind the others in the trial; but Mary's suspense was soon ended. The sniff of disgust, and the outburst of laughter, no longer to be restrained, which answered it from the other victims, was enough; but as none could, as yet, control themselves sufficiently to speak, or reply to her earnest questioning, she was compelled to taste for herself.

"Maggie, Maggie, what have you put into these pies?"

But the girl, who had been restlessly passing in and out of the room, hoping to catch a compliment for her skill, had hastily taken herself off with the first explosion.

"Surely, my dear," said Mr. Herbert, "you did not let that greenest of all green things make your pies?"

"No, indeed; but she set herself to do them, while I was detained by a long call."

"And now do tell us, Mrs. Herbert, what has she put in, or rather what has she *left out?*"

"That is beyond my skill, for such a combination I never heard of. There's *sage* and *pepper* most certainly, salt, and something else I can't make out, and am hardly willing to taste again for the sake of the knowledge."

"The pies were made from the apples of Sodom, I think," said Burgess. "Do call the gipsy, and let's know all about it, just for the fun of the thing."

There was no need of calling, for at that moment

she entered, bundle in hand, and in a towering rage.

"There's no gipsy blood in my veins, I can tell you, sir. And Mister Herbert called me *green;* I'se as good a 'plexion as anybody. And now give me my money."

Mrs. Herbert tried to soothe her; but it was of no avail. There was no forgiveness for the insult of being called gipsy, or for disparaging her complexion, and she left in most sublime indignation.

"Well, I had better look to my bread, or your supper may be as unfortunate as the dessert."

"Oh, *that* was first-rate—perfectly unique—unsurpassed by any French dish in Paris, I dare say. I wouldn't have missed it for anything. Do let us have all the fun you can, and settle the bread question before we go out, for I am hoping that will be of as new a pattern as the dessert," said Stanly, and they laughingly followed her to the kitchen, having received a whispered permission from Mr. Herbert.

"See, it *is* rising beautifully, as the child said. Perhaps she *has* succeeded in this. Poor thing! she thought to do me a favor."

"No doubt of that," replied her husband. "But I want a taste of the bread. Just put a piece on the hot stove, and bake us a 'boy's biscuit.'"

"Well, on one condition—that each of you shall taste a piece, no matter what may be in it."

The "boy's biscuit" was laid on the stove, and its baking watched with much glee. When done, Mrs. Herbert divided it into four parts, and handed a portion to each of the gentlemen.

"But you have reserved none for yourself. Why so generous, my dear?"

"*I* didn't promise to try it, but you did, and I shall hold you to it."

With some hesitation, each took a piece, and far more quickly ejected it, with the most uncouth grimaces.

"We shall never, never forget Lot's wife," said Mr. Herbert.

"Oh, dear! all my bread wasted. Maggie has evidently heard of 'salt risings,' much used out here for yeast, and has given it a very effectual trial."

"Well, we've had a right merry time—better than any dessert you could have provided, Mrs. Herbert."

"Many thanks for taking it so philosophically, young gentlemen."

Some weeks passed, in which Mrs. H. labored unassisted, but was now nearly exhausted. Susie was a quiet, happy little body, but a child of three years must require care, and beside the time drew nigh when her mother would be laid aside from active labor, and she was very anxious to secure some one to relieve her husband from so much toil, and also to make his home rather more comfortable than it had been during some of her illnesses.

At the table one day, Mr. Townly said, "Our unfortunate merry-making, some weeks since, deprived you of a girl, and 'tis but right that we try to secure another. My sister told me this morning that she knew of a colored girl who she thought, in your hands, might become quite useful. Shall I send her, and let you talk with her?"

"I'll answer the question," said Mr. Herbert; "send her, by all means. I know what you would say, my dear, but discipline must be maintained; remember, I have decided that you must rest and take life a little easier; so Townly, send on the 'maid of all work,' (which probably may mean *mistress* of the whole), as soon as you please."

In due time, Sally came; a stout, good-looking yellow-girl.

"Where have you been living?"

"At Massa Baker."

"Why did you leave?"

"Laws me. Misses and the young folks think colored people ain't good enough to wipe feet on, and their pigs live better than they let me. Might as well be a slave again."

"Then you have been a slave? Are you free now?" said Mrs. Herbert.

"Want to send me back, eh!" said the poor girl, with a half-cunning, half-frightened look. "Baker said Massa Herbert ought to be shot, 'cause he is sorry for the slave, and I didn't think, if I came here, you'd be for 'letting on' 'bout me.

"Nor will we, Sally. 'Tis true, we are both very sorry that any one should be held in slavery, and I ask the question from kindness, not from curiosity, or an intention to injure you."

"Then I'se tell you," said she, coming close up to Mrs. Herbert, speaking through her set teeth, 'Ise free *till they catch me*—and I'll die before they do that."

"Well, Sally, if I hire you, what can you do Can you wash and iron?"

"Yes, 'm."

"And keep the house neat and clean?"

"Yes, 'm."

"And do you know anything about cooking?"

"Laws me! sure I do; right handy at it, can cook *anything*, and milk cows, and split wood. Dear me! I can do anything."

"Most too ready at promising," said Mrs. Herbert to herself, "but I may as well try. As I don't expect much, there's no danger of disappointment."

And Sally was engaged to come the next day. At the appointed time she made her appearance. Mrs. Herbert spent the chief part of the forenoon, for several days, with her in the kitchen. She seemed rather inefficient, and not over nice; but as all that had been expected, on the whole, her employers began to flatter themselves that she would, in the end, prove quite as reliable as any assistance they might hope to obtain.

The first evening she had been directed to prepare some chickens for the next day's dinner. When asked if she understood how to do the work correctly, she seemed greatly amused. "Laws sake! Missis think this chile don't know nothing; I can *do po'ltry* nicer nor anything."

Mrs. Herbert felt confident that the girl was not boasting foolishly, in this item of her work, for in a country where game and poultry are so abundant as to be common food for all, surely every one must know all that was needful of the matter; and, quite contented, she sat down to *rest herself* with her needle.

The next day proved that Sally could "dress chickens any how," if she knew nothing else.

For several days, things moved on with some considerable degree of comfort. Sally's want of neatness, which rather increased than diminished, being the most unpromising thing, thus far. But after a while there began to be complaints on the part of Mr. Herbert, corroborated by the other gentlemen, that something was wrong with the coffee.

"Does our new damsel meddle with it? for it tastes like boiled dish towels!"

"Why, George! how can you talk so. Nobody touches the coffee but myself."

"Well, then, my dear, you are losing your skill, most certainly, for it has been growing worse and worse, and now it is past endurance. Does Sally wash the coffee-pot?"

"Yes; but if it were not clean, I should know it when I prepare the coffee."

"Well, then, the tea-kettle, for there's *dirt* somewhere, I'll be bound, as Father Tompkins says."

As soon as breakfast was over, Mrs. Herbert hastened to the kitchen to make a more careful examination. The coffee-pot was all right, but the tea-kettle! Oh, misery! The sediment at the bottom was overpowering; and calling Sally, she inquired how feathers and other garbage came in the tea-kettle!

"Laws sake, missis! and I forgot to *rinse* it after dressing them chickens."

"But what had you to do with the *tea-kettle*, when about such work?"

"'Pears like it heats a sight quicker than 'tother kettle."

Poor Mrs. Herbert thought she had closely kept her eye on everything that passed through Sally's hands, but after such a specimen, she undertook to go over the whole kitchen arrangements, and the result showed such unutterable filthiness, and in places so unheard of before, that Sally was at once dismissed.

The coffee, next morning, was all that could be desired, and when asked what miracle had "healed the bitter waters," and why she was again the sole occupant of the kitchen, Mrs. Herbert replied with a smile:

"'Where ignorance is bliss, 'tis folly to be wise,'

and trust me, the less you know of the matter the better it will be for your digestion."

After two or three weeks had dragged wearily along, Mr. Herbert brought in with him, one afternoon, a smart-looking girl, as black as ebony, of whom a friend had told him, giving her an excellent character for neatness, capacity and good morals.

The next morning, Mrs. Herbert was too ill to do more than sit in her chair, by the kitchen door, and direct. Rose's work was neatly done; no fault could be found with dinner, and all things worked charmingly.

A week from the time Rose came, little Susie was taken, one morning, from her crib, and brought to mamma's bedside, and there lay a tiny little baby brother.

"Oh, mamma! where did you find it?"

"God gave it, my dear."

The child's face settled into a deeply thoughtful expression, and she stood for a moment in silence. Then her countenance flushed, and her blue eyes shone brightly, as though she had solved a question of great moment.

"Oh, I see! God put a rope round little brother, and let him down through the little stars. Now Susie knows what the stars are, little holes right up into God's house; but"—(and a look of intense fear crossed her face)—"oh, mamma, if the rope had broken this morning, and when papa went out he had found the baby all killed to pieces! Oh, dear! oh, dear! how we should have cried, all of us."

"Borrowing trouble already, puss! Rather early to follow the ways of the world," said Mr. Herbert, laughing; and went out to see how Rose was succeeding with breakfast. "Doing *first rate*," was the report; and everything seemed so encouraging, both as regarded the sick one and the kitchen, that Mr. Herbert left soon after morning prayers, saying he should not be home till dinner-time.

Just before dinner, however, Rose looked in and said, "I'm going, missis."

"—Why, Rose!"

"Oh, Missis Allen will give me a quarter more nor you do."

"Well, *I'll* give you the extra quarter, Rose, for you certainly will not leave me when unable to help myself."

Rose departed to her work, and Mrs. Herbert felt quite relieved.

But soon after tea, a neighbor's daughter ran in, and said that Rose had just gone, and requested her to tell Mrs. Herbert that Mrs. Allen had offered her *another quarter* extra, and she left without seeing the missis, "'cause she *knowed* Massa Herbert was not able to give her more than she was already receiving."

"Poor George! what will you do now?" said Mary.

"Far better than the woman who could so tamper with a servant's avarice in times of illness;" and with his usual hopeful and cheerful way, he took upon himself the charge of the next morning's breakfast, making merry over every mistake, and supplying all deficiencies in the cooking, by furnishing food for healthful laughter.

"Now, my dear, the housework is all done up, before Mother Tompkins caught me at it; but as for dressing that small edition of humanity, I have not courage to make the attempt, and shall step over to our good friends and get some of the 'women kind,' to attend to that business, and while they are here, I'll go hunting."

"*Hunting*, George!" exclaimed his wife.

"Yes, *hunting help*."

But the hunt not being successful, the boarders were dismissed. Mr. Herbert attending to the cooking for himself and Susie, while friends took turns in dressing the baby and caring for the mother.

When all was in order, little Susie was commissioned to watch and wait on mamma, while her father left to attend for a short time to parish matters.

And the prim little lady would climb into the most dignified chair she could find, and sit demurely any length of time, brushing flies off from mother and brother, or, in some other way, striving to make herself useful.

With such a gentle nurse, and her husband's loving care, Mrs. Herbert recovered rapidly, and often insisted that she had never been so well cared for in any illness, or so happy, as during those few weeks. And now, more than ever, she was thankful for a small house, as she could get out about her family duties so much easier, and relieve her husband from care more effectually.

And quite too soon for her safety, Mrs. Herbert was again at work, and little Miss Susie raised to the dignity of baby-nurse, an office which she filled with most edifying gravity.

For the remainder of the summer, they were without boarders, although their pecuniary affairs were becoming more and more unsatisfactory; but the garden, under Mr. Herbert's energetic management, was a great assistance, and his wife economized even more rigorously than ever.

CHAPTER XIII.

THE DONATION PARTY.

It is not my intention to follow our friends very minutely, only glancing here and there at a few of the most prominent of their joys and sorrows, blessings and trials. Save that she feared her diminished health might prove a hindrance to her husband's usefulness, Mrs. Herbert would be very unwilling to admit that her lot had fallen on the "shady side" of life. She felt deeply her entire separation from her own family friends, and also that her removal to Norton had cut her off from the society of her husband's brother Frank and his wife. Since leaving Glenville, they had not met, and both herself and husband mourned the loss of their kind coöperation and ready sympathy, more than any deprivation that they had as yet been called to meet. But their affection lost none of its brightness by absence, and many a substantial love token came from this dear sister at just the time of utmost need, which, had it occurred in these more spiritually-developed later days, would certainly have been attributed to the interposition of some "spirit messenger."

When the baby was about three months old, a very dear sister of Mr. Herbert's spent some weeks with them, bringing a little one of the same age with Master Frank. This visit was another of those bright spots, which Mrs. Herbert always loved to recall.

Mrs. Ward, or Sister Agnes, was a woman of very uncommon intellectual attainments, and our Mary thought at first that she should never feel at ease with her. Her warm, loving heart, however, soon dispelled all fears, and the sisters spent many happy hours together, and none more so than those employed each morning in bathing, dressing and administering to the wants of their little pets, and talking over their hopes and fears for the future of the beloved ones committed to their care.

Little Susie was of course a great favorite with her aunty; and her quaint, old-fashioned remarks an unfailing source of amusement.

The young lady, having three months' experience

in "tending the baby," felt quite competent to advise and caution in the management of her young cousin, and the comical air and mock solemnity with which Mrs. Ward would receive her counsels, and draw her out, were irresistibly laughable.

"Now, aunty, it will never do to let little cousin's head hang over your lap so."

"Why not, pussy?"

"Please don't call Susie pussy. Nobody but papa must say that."

"What! not mamma?"

"Oh, no. I'm mamma's little maid."

"Well, and you are Aunt Susie's little quiet mouse, are you not?"

"Mice do mischief, and trouble mamma."

"And that my little utilitarian would not like to do. But, tell me, why may I not let Franky's head fall over my lap? Please explain."

"'Cause Grandma Topsins says it will make babies have *crickets.*"

"Rickets, darling, I presume. But what does that mean?"

"I guess it means *bad tempered;* 'cause she said if brother had them he would cry half the time."

About a week before Mrs. Ward's visit expired, Mrs. Jackson rode over to lay before Mr. and Mrs. Herbert a plan, which, she said, Mrs. Tompkins and some other friends had been arranging, and only waiting for the sanction of their pastor and wife, to carry into execution.

Mrs. Jackson had been undeviating in her kindness, from the hour they had first met, but her rapidly failing health, and the almost constant sickness of some one of her children, prevented her from seeing our friends as often as she wished. Still no festival day passed without seeing the old family carriage, with black Ben, ready to convey Mr. Herbert's people out to "Woodlands," where everybody expected a happy time, and were never disappointed.

The "plan" was an earnest desire on the part of many friends to give a "*donation party.*" "And," said Mrs. Jackson, "I think it can be managed so as to combine much pleasure, with so much of profit as to enable you to pass this winter more comfortably than the last. We wish it very particularly understood, however, that this party, and its proceeds, has nothing to do with your salary. On that you will have just as strong a claim as though no party had been given.

"I am ashamed that your promised support has been so niggardly paid; there is no reason why it should be so. And we desire to give this party, as a strong hint from the ladies, to the gentlemen, of their opinion of the business habits of the church, as well as a proof of our love for, and interest in, you and your family."

She then proceeded to inform them that Mrs. Campbell, Susie's foster-mother, with Mrs. Tompkins and her eldest daughters, would take charge of everything, and were desirous that Mr. Herbert, and his wife and sister, should spend the appointed day at "Woodlands," and give their house in charge to these ladies, promising that everything should be well cared for, and after the party, replaced in "apple-pie order," with no fatigue for Mrs. Herbert.

"There," said Mrs. Ward, laughing, "just look at Mary, brother George. She is perfectly bewildered; and, I'll venture to say, knows nothing about a '*donation party.*'"

"I don't understand why the ladies wish us off all day (though, you know, Mrs. Jackson, it will be a treat to rest at your pleasant home), nor what they mean by *replacing* everything."

"Why, your house is very small, and we shall want your furniture moved out of one room for the tea-table, and one of the little rooms for the 'offering,' and the rest of the house for the guests.

"I see the *housekeeper* all over your face, my dear, and in your heart you are beholding visions of endless confusion."

"Oh, no; you only see that 'tis all a 'muddle' to me. I haven't the least idea *how* it will be; but am grateful for the kindness shown, and certainly have no fears, but our two dear friends, Mrs. Campbell and Mrs. Tompkins, will leave everything in as good, or better condition than they found them. But, Mrs. Jackson, how about my husband's books, table, etc.? They take up full half the room, and I can't see how many people can find place to stand, in the room you have reserved for company."

"Oh, they must all be set out on the veranda."

"*Now look at George's face*, good friends! I appeal to you, if it is not more expressive than mine was a few moments ago. *I* see the anxious student and book-worshipper, in every lineament."

The laugh was fully turned upon Mr. Herbert, who candidly confessed that he should never expect to find book or paper again; but intended to resign himself, with the patience of a martyr, to the infliction.

The next week, on Thursday, was appointed for the visit, and Mrs. Jackson said Ben would be round by eight o'clock of that morning with the carriage.

After Mrs. Jackson left, the subject was fully discussed, and all agreed that, pecuniarily, it would probably not amount to much.

"But," said Mrs. Herbert, "we shall have a good opportunity to see our people, and that never does harm."

"And I shall become better acquainted with them than by a year's common intercourse, and feel a deeper interest; so if in the simple matter of dollars and cents (though I would, by no means be understood to speak disparagingly of *them*), we are no *worse* off, I'm going to be content."

"I am rejoiced," said Mrs. Ward, "that the '*party*' is to come off before I leave; I wouldn't miss it for considerable. I have attended several, and never yet saw one that did not prove a failure.

But there is an efficiency and sincerity about two or three of those who are to have the management of this affair, that will insure success, if anything will. So I shall take great interest in watching the result."

"Well, I am very sanguine, at least, of having a good time—books, papers, and confusion to the contrary notwithstanding," said her brother.

Thursday came at length; a clear, cheerful, October day, and surely there is no month in all the year that can bring such glorious days; in which simply living is such a luxury; no month in which it would be so hard to welcome *death*, and through faith look forward to, and believe in something even more desirable, in the world beyond, as this same bright, beautiful *October*.

And it was on one of her most lovely and invigorating mornings, that Ben drove up before the parsonage, and the merry, blue-eyed Meggie announced that all was ready for their reception at "Woodlands," and that Agnes and Nellie, Jessie and Hattie, with a score of young ladies, were only waiting their departure to step in and help the matrons arrange for the evening's entertainment; while herself and Sister Belle were promised the pleasure of nursing the babies, and playing with Susie. She was, furthermore, instructed to inform the friends, that when all was ready, a carriage would be sent to Woodlands for them; but they were not to approach within hearing distance till then.

A most happy company now entered that commodious old family carriage; care and forethought were for one day dismissed, as they gave themselves up to the luxury of rest, and the full enjoyment of their ride, and anticipations of the novel pleasures of the coming evening.

It was the first time Mrs. Ward had been at "Woodlands," and delighted with the place, and quite in love with her hostess, she felt, with her brother and his wife, that no day had ever passed so quickly or pleasantly away.

At five o'clock the promised carriage arrived for the pastor's family, while Mr. and Mrs. Jackson with their children were to follow in their own conveyance.

On the way, some surprise was expressed that they were sent for at so early an hour, Mrs. Ward remarking, that it was not customary for such parties to begin till after dark. Instead, however, of driving up to their own house, the carriage stopped with them at Mr. Tompkins', where they found Agnes waiting at the gate.

"We want you in here for about an hour."

"Well, Miss Agnes, that's more than we bargained for," said Mr. Herbert, "and I am not at all sure I shall submit to any such encroachments on our freedom."

"But here comes father, and I think you had better yield, 'rescue or no rescue,' for you know he has a trick of picking people up and walking off with them."

"Ah, sis! but it won't do to take such liberties with the Dominie. I haven't forgot, though, how to manage a flock of sheep," said he, jumping little Susie through the carriage window with one hand, and taking the baby from Mrs. Herbert in the other. "There, now I've got the lambs, the old ones will be sure to follow."

When they entered the house, Mrs. Herbert and little Susie were led up-stairs by Mrs. Tompkins, and her husband taken off by the old gentleman, Mrs. Ward being left in the parlor to await further developments.

"You see, we wanted our ministers and his folks to look their best to-night, and reckoned you were somewhat in need of new clothes. Here they are; just you put them on quick. Oh, I can't stop to listen now! Busy times, you know!" and without waiting to see or hear surprise or thanks, he hastily left Mr. Herbert to array himself in an entire new suit from head to foot.

His wife found a similar surprise awaiting her in the chamber to which she was led. A black silk dress and wrought collar, a simple but tasteful head-dress, embroidered handkerchief and white kid gloves, even to the black silk hose and neatly-fitting kid slippers, were all in readiness, and on the table a modest bonnet and substantial shawl.

"They won't bite you," said Mrs. Tompkins, laughing heartily at Mrs. Herbert's bewildered look, and giving her a real motherly kiss.

"Come, we must see how they look. You'll be wanted in half an hour over to *our neighbor's across the way.*"

"How did you find out just what we most needed? and how could you succeed so finely in fitting us?"

"Why, my girls and I have eyes for something beside our own dress, and could see that your garments were getting rather rusty. We know you don't get paid promptly enough to buy all that you really need. As for the fit, Hattie stole (I told her you'd excuse the liberty, I was sure) one of your dresses and a pair of slippers the other day, for patterns. I am only afraid Miss Brady hasn't done the work as neatly as you do yourself. Do you know we've quite an idea of setting up a dress-maker's shop, and appointing you to work for the church?"

"Just to keep you from dying with idleness," said Agnes, coming from the little bedroom adjoining, where she had been busy with Susie.

"But before you engage the shop, Mrs. Herbert, please look at this young lady, and say if Jessie and Nellie Campbell, sister Essie and myself, may not come in as ''prentices,' when mother's plan takes effect?"

"Headworkmen rather, if this is a specimen of your handiwork. Why, Susie, darling, what have they done to you?"

"See, mamma! Aunt Aggie made Susie pretty dress and apron, and new shiny shoes, and what a nice new mamma Grandma Tompkins has made you. But mamma mustn't be proud; *Susie ain't a bit*," said the little gipsy, glancing demurely at the reflection of herself in the mirror, and it may be, that there *was* less of vanity in the bright smile she met there, than of the innate love of beauty, as she saw a fair, sweet face, rich glossy curls, and a trim little figure, most becomingly clad in blue frock and white apron.

"Why, this is fairy-land, my dear; I hardly know myself or you, and wonder if father will."

"Perhaps you won't know him," said Mrs. Tompkins; "but as you are now ready, we will go and see." So saying, Mrs. Tompkins led the way to the parlor.

There the husband and wife were introduced to each other, with great form, and caused much merriment, and at once organized themselves into a "mutual admiration society," and were both so full of self, as not to spare a glance at the "babies," as Mrs. Ward said, showing them little Meggie, in a recessed window, holding both the little ones, dressed precisely alike.

"Only think of my boy's coming in for a share of the donation party."

Their kind friends excused themselves for a moment, so as to be ready to escort them to the parsonage, as soon as the signal should be given.

When left alone, Mr. Herbert said, "Who would have thought, less than a year ago, when we received those lectures on economy, that one day we should have cause to rank this family among our most reliable friends, and be indebted to them for some of our most substantial comforts?"

"I should think their consciences might, by this time, be appeased, for surely they have more than compensated for the two hundred dollars, about which they condemn themselves so severely."

"That's not the only reason why they love and help you, dear sister. The days you devoted yourself to them, when their daughter died, and your dreadful illness in consequence, will never be forgotten."

"Oh, I should probably have been sick anyway. I was well-nigh exhausted before Annie's illness."

"Ah, but the old gentleman has been telling me all about it, while you two were beautifying. I assure you, he has a large, tender heart, under that rough exterior. He wept like a child when he told me how he used to watch outside your door, when you were too ill to see him, and said he, 'If she had died, my woman and I would never have had another happy hour. To think how she wore herself out for us, after all we had said. Ah! it was heaping coals of fire upon our heads, with a vengeance! It almost burns me up sometimes, I tell you, Mrs. Ward.'

"'Well,' said I, 'I should think you were in a fair way to extinguish the "coals," if you are always in the practice of throwing on such "*dampers*" as you have been doing since I came in town. I know they look upon you as their best and dearest friends.'

"'Well, now! Do tell! *Is* that so? Then I'm happier than I ever expected to be, since my Annie died.'"

They were now wanted at the scene of the evening's festivities. When they entered their own door, fresh surprises awaited them. All that was familiar had vanished; bed, table, books, etc. A pretty carpet covered the floor (a luxury they had never possessed), a nice, chintz-covered, comfortable lounge, fitting in under one of the front windows, a large, cane-seated rocker, half a dozen chairs to match, a little chair for Susie, and a handsome clock on the mantel.

"There, this is all you can be allowed to see just

at present," said Mrs. Campbell; "the guests will soon arrive, and I have a cover which I must put over this carpet, before they come; it will take but a minute, and you must be all ready to play hostess. We now resign that place to you, and will only retain the charge of the supper, and placing such gifts as are not handed immediately to you, in the little room destined for them."

A long, four-seated wagon was the first to halt before the little gate, and land its troop of old and young.

"Good Elder Fairchild, and his dame, with their flock," said Mrs. Campbell, and Mr. and Mrs. Herbert came forward to welcome them; and then the old lady, as she kissed Mrs. Herbert, said:

"*I* only bring a small token of love, the elder has sent the substantials round to the back door; and she handed a pair of most excellent yarn stockings for each of the family, even to the gossamer worsted ones for little Frank, spun and knit by her own hands.

Her daughters, one twelve and the other fifteen, gave a patchwork spread, beautifully quilted, which they had put together themselves. The two youngest placed in Susie's hands a basket filled with fancy cakes of maple-sugar, and in another basket a pair of little white chickens.

Bill, meanwhile, under Mrs. Campbell's direction, had driven round, and was handing out a large bag of flour, a barrel of splendid fall apples, a jug of country molasses, and a jar of butter, so pure and golden that Mrs. Campbell insisted on bringing it into the parlor; "for," said she, "as there is no one but the givers here, I couldn't think of mixing it with more that may be sent in, before our pastor and his wife have seen it. Mrs. Fairchild's butter is famous all over the State."

And surely never was such butter seen.

"I think," said Mr. Herbert, "my wife will at last acknowledge that she has seen butter in the West, that *nearly* equals her own mother's. That is a compliment you would be proud of, Mrs. Fairchild, if I could just transport you to the 'Hill Farm,' where I wooed my wife."

"I'm sure I shall be greatly pleased, if my butter reminds her of her mother in connection with myself. But hurry it off to the pantry, Mrs. Campbell, for here come other friends."

To save confusion and embarrassment, Mrs. Campbell had just nailed a card to the front gate, requesting that the eatables, and heavier gifts, might be taken to the rear entrance, where some one was stationed to receive and label each article, that the giver might be recognized when the gifts were examined.

Dr. Marvel and lady soon entered, and shaking hands gravely, the doctor offered Mr. Herbert a *pill-box* as his gift. Amidst much laughter, he begged to decline. The doctor pretended to feel quite slighted, and declared that Mrs. Herbert was too much of a lady to refuse a poor fellow's gift, however trifling. A quick glance from Mrs. Marvel was as quickly understood, and, when the box was offered, she took it with many thanks and a profound courtesy.

"Ah!" said her husband, "my wife was a *physician's* daughter, and probably has a more kindly appreciation of the gift than I can be expected to have."

"And you, sir, being a *clergyman*, can perhaps understand what virtue there may be in these," said our old friend Mr. Upton, presenting a set of theological works. "I'm sure they are all Greek to me."

"Oh! just what I was longing for, and most

hopelessly, the very last time I was in Stanley's book-store. Notwithstanding they are Greek to you, friend Upton, I trust you will not doubt they are most acceptable to me."

"Are you afraid of opening that pill-box, Mrs. Herbert?" said Upton, laughing.

"Oh, no! I've enjoyed a peep at it, all by myself. My husband has no curiosity, but all who will, may share with me in *looking*, but not *handling* or *tasting*;" and opening the box, she displayed a number of gold pieces, which, when Mr. Herbert saw, he assured her he was on the instant struck with illness, which only such medicaments could remove.

A handsome box of knives from Townly, and a plain, white dining set from Stanly, and a pretty china tea-set from Burgess, their old boarders, induced Mrs. Campbell to tell them "they were *hinting* a wish to return to their old table comforts again."

"Rather, I think," said their former hostess, smiling, "betraying a knowledge that the table *conveniences* were rather limited."

"No breach of confidence, I trust," said Stanly

"If it is," said Mr. Herbert, "we certainly feel

more 'honored in the breach than in the observance.'"

We will not stop to comment on each new arrival, or the many sportive remarks between the givers and receivers. In a short time the house was filled to its utmost capacity.

About nine o'clock, supper was announced. The ladies had found it necessary, as the parsonage was too small, to spread their table in an empty tenement belonging to the premises, only a step from the house, and the guests were requested to follow the pastor and his lady at once to the room, where they found such a table as none but real *western* hospitality could spread. It would take too much space to attempt a minute description. Tea and coffee, which neither China nor France could surpass; the richest of cream, in no stinted measure. Every imaginable kind and form of cake, pies, bread, biscuit, and sweetmeats. Ham, tongue, turkey, chickens, birds and game—baked meats, ornamented with every fancy that the genius of cookery could devise were there, most tastefully decked with vines and flowers.

The supper passed off without a shadow to mar the enjoyment. Even the little folk, for once, had no cause to complain that they were overlooked, or had not an opportunity to taste all, and as much as their parents would allow.

From the table they returned to the parsonage, and the following hymn, written for the occasion, was sung:

FOR THE

DONATION VISIT TO REV. GEORGE HERBERT.

AIR—*Ariel.*

In social harmony we meet—
With heart and hand each other greet,
In friendship's warm embrace;
Thankful for common mercies shared—
Nor less to meet, as we are spar'd,
In this thrice-happy place.

Not from the well-springs of the heart,
Should joy's full streams flow on apart,
But mingle into one;—
The generous vine supported lives,
Strengthened by the embrace it gives,
In either shade or sun.

Pastor and people here convene,
And mingle in one grateful scene
Of thankfulness and joy;
And while with gifts our hands are stor'd,
Our hearts unite, with full accord,
In love without alloy.

When "in one place, with one accord;"
As the disciples of our Lord
 In ancient times were met,
The Spirit came, with mighty power—
And the brief record of that hour
 Inspires his followers yet.

The age of miracles is past—
But love divine will always last,
 And love from man to man;
The heart, warm'd by the Spirit's flame,
In every age abides the same,
 Through one all-glorious plan.

"Love never fails"—but e'er abides—
And, join'd with duty, well provides—
 For laborers faithful found;
Sure, then, our task must pleasure be
Now to reward fidelity,
 With genius richly crown'd.

Mr. Herbert then offered a fervent prayer, and with many kind words the company gradually departed, leaving behind them and carrying with them tenfold more love for each other than they had ever felt before.

As their friends were leaving, it was not strange that the thought should cross Mrs. Herbert's mind, "How are we ever to put our rooms in order, so as to be able to sleep to-night, and now past 11 o'clock?"

The beds, furniture, etc., had been placed in the back yard, and the books on the veranda. But she soon saw that the *managers* were not intending to leave their work half done.

A kind hint, kindly taken, dispersed all who were not needed for effectual service. Four or five ladies and a dozen gentlemen remained, and, refusing any assistance from the family, were at once busy in "*repairing damages*," as Townly said.

In an inconceivably short time, the beds were up and made, and little Susie and the babies snugly sleeping in their appropriate resting-places. Books, as if by magic, walked back into their proper nooks, and in less than an hour one could hardly realize what lively scenes had just been passing there.

As the young gentlemen said good night, one of their number, in the name of the whole, presented Mr. Herbert with a pocket-book, and good Mother Tompkins said, "all is in order, except the sweeping. We've had girls at work *doing up dishes*, and putting away the food, and in the morning you will only have to place the articles to suit yourself. Each lady has carried home with her all her own dishes, and you will have nothing to send back.

Some of us will see you in the course of the day—to-morrow. Good night." And with the warm thanks and true love of their pastor's family, the good mothers in Israel departed.

The parcel handed by the young man contained fifty dollars.

"And now, sister Susan, do you call this party a failure?" said Mr. Herbert, when the last guest had departed.

"Certainly not, as far as enjoyment goes, for I have never spent a more delightful evening."

"And I am sure," said Mary, "you can't call the gifts a failure. Their pecuniary value, judging only from the little I have seen, is fourfold more than I dreamed of."

"Well, I shan't decide about that till I've seen all. The fact is, I must confess to a large share of Eve's curiosity. I doubt if I can sleep well till I take a peep into the pantries and that little bedroom. Are you sleepy, Mary?"

"Not a bit."

"Nor you, George?"

"No, not I. I'm perfectly ready for an exploring expedition. We'll take the pantries first."

The flour, meal, pork, ham, chickens, eggs, and

butter and vegetables, were of no trifling value. As for the cooked food, Mrs. Ward said they would have to make a party every day in the week, and invite the town, in order to save it.

In the little room were several pieces of flannel, of various qualities, lengths and colors. Two webs, or "cuts," as they were called, of bleached cotton, two delaines, and three calico dresses for Mrs. Herbert, several for the children. Gloves, hosiery, thread, pins, needles, tape, and something of almost every article that seamstress or housekeeper could ask for, which, together with the new suits which they had on, the parlor furnishing and the money, Mr. Herbert calculated would amount to more than two hundred dollars.

"What an assistance this party will prove," said Mary. "And then to be relieved from the painful necessity of bringing our affairs before our people, and insisting upon the prompt payment of our promised support, or being compelled to leave just as we have begun to love them. This kindness will, at least, enable us to defer the evil day, and to settle two or three bills, which have mortified me exceedingly."

"Ah, sister! have you already become so

acclimated as to be content to *defer* the evil day?"

"No, indeed! anything but *content;* but is it not best, when all your efforts will not overcome an evil, to try and *hope* that, while you endeavor to endure it patiently, something more potent than your feeble struggles may come in by and by, and remove it altogether. I hardly dare hope it, and yet, there is so much of real good feeling, so much *heart* among this people, that they only need some *shock* to *rouse* them to the sense of their duty, and that once done, I do not fear their settling down into thoughtlessness again."

"Perhaps the *only* thing that will do *that,* may be the loss of a minister whom they love so well, as I have not a doubt they do brother George."

"*That* would be as painful to us as it could be to them," said Mr. Herbert; "but if that is the *only way,* then there is this comfort, that whoever takes my place will be benefited by their waking up."

"I doubt it. But if the money you have received to-night must go to pay debts, which their remissness has compelled you to contract, when these provisions are exhausted, will the influence of this party be, to make your people more prompt in their future payments; or rather, will it not be used as an excuse for greater remissness in future? That was what I feared when the party was first proposed. It has been the effect of all that have come within my knowledge. How will it be with your people?"

"Well," said Mr. Herbert, somewhat sadly, "I fear our people will prove no exception. Those who have the charge of the monetary affairs of the church, had nothing to do with this pleasant day, and, I noticed, were not among the callers, even. The whole thing has been planned and executed by warm personal friends, who would gladly give us double the salary we now have, and pay us promptly, if they '*were to the fore.*'"

"Then, why don't *they* make a commotion, and place the management in the hands of those who will do their duty."

"Why? Just because they don't like to seem to interfere—don't like trouble, etc. Excepting good old Father Tompkins, they have the true western dislike of any extra exertion, and *trust to time to bring all right.* They are energetic enough in making money, but have serious objections to any self-sacrifice of ease or quiet, for other people, especially for the support of preaching. It is a great fault of character in this country, though one which, I think, will change as the country grows older; but it will not be in my day, however. There are scores of ministers worse paid than I am; but those who come after us will reap the fruit of our toil and self-denial.

"But for this one night, I will 'hang care,' and forget, as long as I can, in the memory of the pleasure we have just enjoyed, the perplexities which will make themselves heard soon enough, I dare say. At any rate, the kindness this day manifested was *real and from the heart*, and we will overlook the faults and short-comings of some, in the sincere love and good intentions of others. And now, good night."

CHAPTER XIV.

A WELCOME VISIT AND A SAD PARTING.

A FEW weeks after the "donation visit," a very dea: friend and relative of Mrs. Herbert came from the East, to reside for some time in her family. It was a rich treat to see an old, familiar face, and to be able to ask those endless questions of home and its inmates, which can never be asked, or answered satisfactorily, by writing.

Helen Mason had spent some weeks at Dr. Leighton's just before leaving the East.

She was an orphan, and almost like a child to Mrs. Leighton, and had been as a sister to Mary before her marriage. Mary's parents were now alone, their children scattered all over the land. Harry and John were both in college, though the latter's health, it was feared, would prevent his completing his education in a manner satisfactory to himself.

Harry was on his last year at college, and would, immediately after leaving, enter upon the study of medicine.

It was sad to think of her parents left solitary in the evening of life; but Helen assured her she had never seen them happier, though the doctor was less active than in former years.

In the pleasant society of her husband, aided by her cousin's busy fingers, the winter and spring passed more pleasantly in many respects than the last, though darkened somewhat by the old trouble of non-payment, and the fear of being eventually compelled to leave, on that account. They were determined to put off that day as long as possible, for though they felt how utterly inexcusable, not to say dishonest, such laxity was, yet their hearts clung very closely to their people, notwithstanding all, and they shrunk with intense pain from the bare idea of leaving them.

Mr. Herbert was rapidly growing in the estimation, not only of the inhabitants of Norton, but his talent and influence were becoming widely known and appreciated throughout the State. *Protracted meetings* were common, and on those occasions *he* was invariably sought after, and was often absent weeks at a time. His people were very proud of his popularity, or, as Mr. Upton, in his outspoken manner, often told them, "were very ready to show off his '*good points,*' but never willing to pay for them, excepting in words, and some of these days they would receive their reward, by seeing some church walk off with their "Dominie,' who could just as highly appreciate, and were more ready to compensate labors performed."

Very many applications had been already made and quietly declined, though Cousin Helen once told him she intended to report every one she could hear of, and try if that would not *scare* the people of Norton into seeing the folly of expecting him to labor without remuneration. But Mr. Herbert always said: "No, if honor and a sense of justice can't induce them to do their duty, I certainly shall not attempt to influence them through fear or selfishness."

Late in the spring, Mrs. Jackson began to show symptoms of decline. She had taken a sudden cold, and was now confined to her bed, with little hope of recovery. Mr. and Mrs. Herbert saw her almost every day, and were pained at the rapid failure of her strength.

Dr. Marvel trusted at first, if she lingered till June, she might rally, for some months at least, but now there seemed little hope of that.

Mrs. Herbert had never realized, till now, how much she had depended on this tried friend, for sympathy and comfort at all times. She was ever gentle and unobtrusive, and there was a charm about her that won all hearts.

One warm, cheerful morning, Mr. Herbert came home from a visit to their sick friend, and reported that the last few days of settled warm weather had produced a most wonderful effect upon her, so much so that her family were feeling encouraged, and she had herself admitted that she felt equal to an old-fashioned visit from her pastor's family. He had therefore promised that they would come to dinner, and spend the day. Ben was to be round for them in an hour or two.

Mrs. Herbert appeared troubled, fearing it would be too much for her friend; "and besides," said she, "this sudden rallying frightens me."

"If it were not so warm, and so near June, I

should myself be greatly alarmed; but whatever may be the result of her present comfortable state, she has set her heart on this visit, and her family are unwilling she should be disappointed. You can easily judge if the excitement is likely to injure her, and if so, we can leave at any time. None of us need be in her room any longer than she can see us without fatigue; and aside from Mrs. Jackson's urgency, one thing that induced me to consent to the arrangement was the worn, dispirited looks of Jessie and Hattie. They have been so long confined, and have suffered so much anxiety for their mother, that I thought a little cheerful society might be beneficial."

Ben came promptly, and soon conveyed them to the pleasant home at Woodlands. To Mrs. Herbert's surprise, they found the invalid sitting up, and looking so bright and lovely, that Cousin Nellie could not realize that there was any danger. But to the more experienced eyes which were watching her, it was a loveliness most intensely painful. She received them with all her usual gentleness, and more than the usual affectionateness, saying, she could not have borne the disappointment, had they not come.

After a short time, the gentlemen went out for a walk, and the daughters took Helen and the children into the garden, leaving Mrs. Herbert with their mother. The friends conversed freely, for some time, recalling their first meeting, and all the way they had been led to their present friendship. A short silence ensued, each too busy with thought, for words. At length, Mrs. Jackson took Mary's hand, and looking earnestly into her face, said—

"What do *you* think of my case? *You*, surely are not deceived, with the rest of my dear ones, by this revival of strength?"

The suddenness of the question quite startled her friend, and before she could reply, Mrs. Jackson added:

"It was for this I wished so much to see you, but fear I may have taxed your friendship too far. You need not reply to my question, dear Mrs. Herbert; I know that my days are numbered. I shall not live a week; I do not think I shall see another rising sun. But my poor husband and children are sadly deceiving themselves with false hopes, which, to my surprise, Dr. Marvel does not discourage. I have not the strength or heart to tell them that I am *dying*. Will not you and Mr. Herbert tell them the truth? And the sooner after dinner, the better for them, poor things!"

"What makes you think so, dear Mrs. Jackson? You look so much better, your voice is clearer, and in every way, you seem stronger than I have known you for weeks."

"Ah! dear friend, my disease is a deceitful one; but I am thankful that I am not myself blinded by it. In this sudden increase of strength, I read a warning to set my house in order immediately, and with my lamp trimmed, and burning, be ready for the bridegroom, at any moment.

"'I see a hand you cannot see,
It beckons me away.'

"Do not weep for me. All is peace, and I think I am ready to depart; only my poor, weak heart shrinks from saying this to my loved ones, and coward-like, I have laid the burden on you."

"Oh! do not say so. My husband and myself will gladly spare you any pain—but"—

"But *you know*, my friend, that I am not mistaken. I saw it in your startled look, and pallid face, when you entered my room. I think your husband understands it also, for his prayer with me this morning was that of a faithful pastor, by a *death-bed.* Oh, you have both been such blessings to me and mine! Do you know, Meggie yesterday told me she thought she had found the Saviour, and now as my last lamb is gathered into the fold, I am willing to leave them all with the good Shepherd, and go home to rest and heaven."

Poor Mrs. Herbert! It was a hard task to go out to that hospitable board, where she had so often sat with its gentle mistress, bearing in her heart such a message, and yet bound to conceal it till they had taken the last cheerful meal together, they would probably know for a long time. But she bore her part in the conversation so calmly, that not even her husband perceived she was concealing anxiety, under a quiet exterior.

As soon as she left the table, she stepped aside with Mr. Herbert, and told him of Mrs. Jackson's request. She found him less surprised than she had been, and also learned that, while walking with Mr. Jackson, he had intimated to him what he feared. They thought it best to return at once to the family, when Mr. Herbert would, as gently as possible, inform them what was so much to be apprehended.

Very tenderly was this most painful of all duties, which falls to a pastor's lot, performed.

And deeply did Mr. Jackson grieve, and bitter were the tears shed by those loving children, for, though they had long feared this, when was ever the heart prepared to yield up its treasures? When did Death ever find friends ready for his immediate approach? But he was nearer to the sorrowing group than any imagined, save the one for whom they mourned. She was not surprised, or taken unawares.

While they sat weeping over their pastor's communication, they were hastily summoned to the sick-room. She still sat where Mrs. Herbert had left her, but oh! how changed! The bright rose tint had fled from her cheek, the death damps were on her brow; but the eye still shone with unutterable tenderness, and the old, familiar, and most beautiful smile, still hovered about her lips.

"Thanks, dear friends! Your message was delivered none too soon. I am going fast, and so happy! My dear husband—my precious children!"

One gasp—an instant's struggle—and she has safely passed the dark river, and

"Life's fever fit is o'er."

Little Maggie, with a scream, threw herself at her mother's feet, and buried her face in her lap, and the rest stood, stricken dumb, or paralyzed by the suddenness of the blow.

Mr. Herbert knelt a moment by the side of the dear saint, and poured out a prayer for comfort and support; then rising, took her gently in his arms, and laid her on the bed, while Mrs. Herbert, approaching, closed those eyes, that but a moment before were beaming with love on the sad weepers around her; then taking her husband's arm, passed silently out, leaving the family alone with their dead! Poor Mary! the daughters could hardly have felt more truly bereaved.

Mr. Herbert left her for a short time, to procure such assistance as was needed, and then returned to report to Mr. Jackson, and offer any other service, in his power to render.

He found his wife comforting, by her silent sympathy and tenderness, the sorrowing family, and Mr. Jackson thanked him with tears for the relief from present arrangements, which his thoughtful kindness had afforded him.

While they were yet speaking, a carriage drove rapidly to the door, and the driver hurriedly inquired for Mr. and Mrs. Herbert. Instinctively, all felt that some other trial was near.

"Mrs. Tompkins was taken ill last night, and Dr. Marvel now thinks cannot live an hour. She is exceedingly anxious to see you both, immediately."

It was a terrible shock to all. "Why," said Mr. Herbert, "it was only at sunset last evening, that I stood with her at the gate, and she seemed as well and cheerful as ever."

Cousin Helen and the children were called, and the pastor and his family turning, with heavy hearts, from these dear friends, were soon on their way to the probable death-bed of another of their best and truest supporters.

Few words were spoken, for Mary, who had struggled bravely with her tears while at Mr. Jackson's, could no longer restrain them, and her kind husband, feeling that it would be a relief, and enable her more calmly to meet the trial in prospect, allowed her to weep unrestrainedly for some minutes.

But as they drew near the house, which had been to them a second home, he laid his hand fondly on hers, saying:

"My dear wife, try now to compose yourself, that we may, to the best of our abilities, comfort the stricken friends to whom we go. It is very, very trying; but my Mary will forget her own grief for a time, to soothe and support those who must be even more deeply afflicted."

"Yes, dear. But, oh! George, these last few hours are so like a horrible dream."

"We shall find it a sad reality, and must look for strength from on high. Vain is the help of man, and never more truly realized, than in such dark hours as these."

Nellie and the children went directly to the parsonage, but Mr. and Mrs. Herbert entered the house of mourning, and were met at the door by Dr. Marvel.

"Is there any hope?" asked Mr. Herbert.

"Not a shadow! You must hasten. She has taken leave of husband and children, and I think the spirit lingers only for you, to find release from the most terrible sufferings I ever witnessed. She is easier now, but just gone!"

They passed quietly to her bedside. What a change in one short day! But, oh! how full of love unutterable was the smile with which she greeted them! Taking both their hands, and carrying them to her cold lips, she said, feebly:

11

"I waited but for this. In an hour least expected the summons came, but I trust it found me not unprepared. Bless you, my dear children, for such you are to me. To your friendship and love, my daughter, and your faithful teachings, my dear son, I owe the happiest and purest days of my life. I leave my poor husband to your tenderness, and gentle ministrations, for the few days that separate us; and my children—you will not cease to pray for, and watch over them. God comfort and bless you all!"

A shadow passed over her face—the light faded from her eye, the feeble breath grew fainter and fainter.

"She is gone," said Dr. Marvel; but suddenly she opened her eyes—the films of death lifting for a moment, she looked lovingly on each sad face, and tried to speak; but again darkness encompassed her, and after a short, faint struggle, Mary, for the second time that day, closed the eyes of one, who had been to her a blessing and support. How much she had loved, trusted and leaned upon her, as an unfailing friend, she had never realized till now.

The death of two, so widely known, and highly

esteemed, cast a shadow over the whole community. They were among the first settlers of the town, coming to take up their abode there, when one store, a log church, and four log cabins were all that constituted the village.

Mrs. Jackson's death had been long expected; and though sudden at last, the shock could not be as severe as Mrs. Tompkins' removal had occasioned. But a day before, and she was, to all appearances, well, and none seemed more sure of many years, of health and usefulness.

She was attacked late at night, with a *chill*, which terminated in congestion.

The next Sabbath, the day appointed for the two funerals, was one long to be remembered. Few who were present will ever forget their pastor's sermon, and the strong affection he so freely and publicly manifested for both the departed ones, made it even more impressive. He had felt all the morning that it would be only by a great effort that he could go through the services, it was so like preaching a mother's funeral sermon. But when he ascended the pulpit, and saw before him those two coffins—the double loss, to himself and wife, aside from grief for the weeping families, before him, overcame him for a moment, and he bowed his head upon the Bible before him, to hide emotion he could not suppress.

I will dwell no longer on this part of my narrative. Each reader can imagine such a burial far better than I can describe, and the return to two such homes, made desolate. To Mr. and Mrs. Herbert the loss was irreparable, and thoug hmany, very dear, yet remained, none were ever found to fill the places in their hearts, which these beloved friends had occupied.

CHAPTER XV.

A JOURNEY.

We will pass lightly over the record of the next year, marked by no incident which will materially increase whatever interest may be found in these pages, but filled with those little corroding cares and anxieties that eat away health, and courage, like a canker. Labor beyond the strength, the closest management and increasingly poor pay, are things which do not make any great *sensation* in a story, but they fill early graves as surely as broken hearts or disappointed affections; and it was such cares which were withering the roses on Mary's cheek, and making her husband prematurely old.

Mrs. Herbert's failing health was a source of great sorrow to her husband, and of no little uneasiness to herself. The chills and fever, which had afflicted her for more than two years, had severely tried her naturally fine constitution, and now there were indications which led them to fear serious affection of the lungs.

Her cousin's presence with them had been a most invaluable assistance and blessing. She was a charming girl, very lovely in person, and in character still more attractive. Always cheerful, and never idle, she was one of the very few persons who can reside for any length of time in a family, and never be a *restraint.*

She had been with them some months, when certain *calls* began to wear a somewhat suspicious character. Mr. Francis was a business man of the place, somewhat older than Mr. Herbert, but an intimate friend. Within the year, he, together with a large number, of whom Helen was one, united with the church. He was a man whom most would call eccentric, and not very likely to be a general favorite; but possessing many sterling traits of character, calculated to attach those who understood him very strongly, and when once they had learned to judge him by his heart, his peculiarities were sources of perpetual amusement, rather than any annoyance.

Mr. and Mrs. Herbert had fancied him from the first, and a warm friendship had sprung up between them; but they were quite taken by surprise when they learned that there was a stronger feeling than friendship in his regard for Helen.

Like an honorable man, he applied to those who were her most natural advisers and guardians, before in any way intimating his wishes to the lady. When their astonishment would allow them to think calmly, they frankly told him that his age was their only objection, and if Miss Helen could overlook that, certainly no one else need be troubled by it.

With their permission, therefore, he proceeded at once to make known his feelings to their cousin, in a frank and manly manner. To her it was as unexpected as to her friends, but she had long known him, and once known, it was not hard for one so persevering to teach her to love as well as esteem.

Of course their engagement gave rise to a great variety of remarks, of little consequence to any, and certainly of none to the parties concerned.

Mr. Francis was earnest, but very reasonable, and felt that he ought not to urge an early day for their marriage, on Mrs. Herbert's account. Another son had, within a few weeks, been added to their number, and as the mother continuing more than usually weak, her cousin determined to remain with her some months longer, and take a larger amount of care upon herself, by way of making experiments in housekeeping.

When Mrs. Herbert was able to go out a little, she was urged to spend a week or two with her husband at his brother Frank's. A revival being in progress among his people, George's assistance, in a series of meetings, was very desirable. All her friends were urgent that the visit should be made, and Helen said:

"You will never have a better time; for it is not always that you will be able to leave your family in such competent hands."

But, though she greatly desired to go, none knew so well as herself, that they ought not to spare the money necessary to take them to Stanwood, and home again.

To Mr. Francis' credit, he was the first to suspect the true reason, and one evening, as he was leaving, said:

"Mrs. Herbert, you'll go with your husband, to-morrow, I'm sure. It don't take you long to get ready for any movement; and Helen, I think, can give you some new reasons in favor of the journey, which you have not yet taken into consideration."

"I can't imagine what they can be, for I thought all that could be said had been exhausted long ago. I need no urging, and if I consulted my wishes only, I should not hesitate, I assure you. But I honestly feel that I ought not to go, and here's my good husband (much as he wishes it) dare not tell me that it would be right to do so."

"Well, don't be too sure. If Helen's reasons don't outweigh yours, I'll give it up. Good night."

"Well, Helen," said Mr. Herbert, as Mr. Francis closed the door, "what are the wonderful reasons? I am sure I shall be under infinite obligations to your friend, if they are such as Mary will think sufficient to justify her accompanying me."

"They are not so wonderful as substantial," said she, handing Mary some gold pieces. "Here are thirty *bright* reasons at any rate, even if they do not prove *strong* ones, and the offer from Mr. Francis of the loan of a fine horse and buggy, if you will go. If not, you can't have either the money or the conveyance. What have you to say now?"

"Nothing, but to thank your friend most heartily. My only objection was the expense."

"What a husband you will have, cousin Nell! You ought to be proud of him. I hear daily of just such acts, secretly performed; but these deeds of kindness will creep out. He can't conceal them always."

The journey was deferred one day, that Mary need not be hurried. The first part of their route took them across the same road they had passed when they came to Norton, and at first they could not but think sadly of the many changes, since that time. But the freedom from care, and the pleasure anticipated in meeting once more the dear brother and sister to whom they were going, soon dispelled all sadness, and they both entered into the full enjoyment of the ride, with the enthusiastic relish of young children.

"This is entirely a new experience for us, my dear Mary," said Mr. Herbert. "It makes me feel quite boyish. If I could see a little more color in those pale cheeks, and you'd just put the baby into your travelling-basket, I could almost imagine I was taking that first ride, in the early days of our courtship, over the dear old Massachusetts hills."

"You will have to shut your eyes before you can well imagine anything like our *home hills* in this flat, boggy region, and with you eyes closed, you can, at the time, forget my baby and pale face, and give me a specimen of some of those fine speeches you used to make. I should quite enjoy, and no doubt be better able to appreciate them, than in the olden times."

"Ah! here we are 'stalled' completely. I must defer my complimentary speeches, and request your ladyship to alight, while I search for rails to pry our wheels up to 'terra firma' once more."

A peculiar feature in western travelling, is the deep mud or "slew holes," which often occasion teamsters and travellers much annoyance. As in the present instance, the road gives no indication of deeper mud in one spot than another, when, without any apparent change, you find your carriage sinking up to the hubs in deep, black mud, as adhesive as wax.

After many ineffectual attempts, George succeeded in raising the wheels so as to rest them, somewhat, on the rails he had used for levers, and Mary, with her child in her arms, took hold of the bridle, to encourage Charley to make one grand effort, while his master tugged at the wheel, and by their united exertions, succeeded at last in gaining mud of a more comfortable depth.

"A very pleasant little episode, by way of variety," said Mr. Herbert, when they were again under way; "but I shall be obliged to let all love-making alone, Mary, dear, till we are through 'Black Swamp,' and attend more carefully to my horse. It was all my own fault, getting into difficulty this time."

"I'm sure I don't see how you make that out. I saw no difference. The road appears *all mud*, and no worse at that point than anywhere else."

"But don't you perceive that the *tracks* all pass round that particular spot, showing it to be a troublesome, if not impassable place? I have had too much experience in such things, not to have known better than to have been caught as I was. But we are over the worst of our journey; and though early in the afternoon, shall be obliged to stop at the next hotel. We cannot reach the second till too late for safe travelling over these roads. I am sorry, for the first tavern is a poor one."

"It is moonlight, and I have no fears, with you

for a driver. A ride after sunset will be delightful, I think; certainly far preferable to an uncomfortable resting-place for the night."

"Thank you for your confidence in my skill; but if we go on, we shall have some ten miles after dark, without passing a single house; and a break-down would be rather inconvenient, or a night spent in a bog-hole, more disagreeable than a dirty house, and not quite as safe for Master Harry. See, Charley smells his oats, and yonder is the 'house of entertainment for man and beast.'"

"What, that large two-story new house? I have not seen so imposing a building since we left home. We shall surely find comfortable quarters here, and you have been slandering it, just to tease me. At your old tricks. You have indeed gone back to your younger days," said Mary, sportively.

"We shall soon see. I only speak from report, having never tried it myself."

They were shown into a large room, with two beds. The front door opened at once into it, without any hall, or entrance, and the "bar," in a recessed corner, opposite the door, was the most prominent object in the room.

Leaving Mary here, Mr. Herbert went to see after the comfort of his faithful horse, saying he would soon return, and make arrangements for a room, where she could wash and rest awhile before supper.

Mrs. Herbert thought she had had some knowledge of these country "places of entertainment;" but for dirt and discomfort, this was far beyond her experience. Several vulgar, profane men were at the bar, some smoking, some drinking, and all of them boisterous. Three or four forlorn-looking children were romping about the room, peering into the travellers' faces, and asking all manner of impertinent questions. That could have been overlooked, but their unkempt hair, torn and filthy garments, and faces that looked as though water was an unknown article, were exceedingly disgusting and almost intolerable.

Several other travellers had alighted from the stage just as our friends drove up, and were seated, quite at home, on beds, chairs, or stools, as they fancied.

"Well, Mary," whispered her husband, "what do you think of this 'imposing house,' thus far?"

"Not much, if this is the best of it. But you

see this room is public property. Perhaps we shall find our apartments more prepossessing, and the table may prove quite tolerable for hungry travellers. But I see no "*woman-kind*" about the establishment. That sad, ghost-like looking Mr. Allison, is, apparently, host, hostess, and all."

Mr. Herbert left her to inquire about a room, but soon returned, with a comical expression which contrasted rather suspiciously with his words.

"You are partly right, my dear. Our apartments *are* rather imposing; but we will defer a visit to them till after supper, which is nearly ready."

"But, George, I want to wash and put myself and baby a little to rights, before trying to eat. Can't I see the landlady?"

"Oh! you and Harry are as clean as you will be after washing, I assure you, and quite as likely to relish your supper now, as after you have been to your room. As for the landlady, she is 'snoring drunk' in that little room off there. No wonder Mr. Allison looks disheartened and wretched. It is said he is a 'right clever fellow,' and would do well if his wife did not paralyze all his efforts by her outrageous habits. A little one, not older than ours, lies in a cradle by her side, a most loathsome and forlorn object."

Supper was announced, and they followed into a long, cold, cheerless apartment, unutterably dirty, where the table was spread. A cloth, ragged and unwashed, covered the rough boards that had been nailed together by no skillful hand, and dignified with the name of table; and the food—could any degree of hunger make that palatable? It might be, but Mrs. Herbert had not yet reached the proper stage of starvation.

"Shut your eyes and open your mouth, and make an effort, my dear," whispered her husband.

Meats of various kinds were passed, but some foreign ingredient in each compelled Mary to decline, however reluctant to distress the poor landlord by so doing. Some biscuit which could only be compared to balls of dried putty—honey, black as tar, garnished with the wings and bodies of the industrious little manufacturers—and the butter, how could she venture upon that?

"A cup of tea, if you please."

It was brought, and the milk-pitcher and black maple sugar placed before her. The sugar she declined, but poured some milk into her tea. The instant it touched the hot liquid, it rose in a thick curd to the top!

Mr. Herbert, meanwhile, who sat by her side, pretended to be busy with the preparation of his own food; but was in reality roguishly enjoying the increasing hopeless expression of his wife's face. At last he said:

"Take a boiled egg, Mary, no dirt *can* find its way inside of that; and really this ham looks quite inviting. Come, try it, dear, *I* never saw the food yet, that I could not manage to eat of, and you will be obliged to learn the same lesson, if you travel much in this country, I assure you."

The ham she declined, perceiving, at the moment, an appendage to the piece on her husband's plate, which effectually destroyed all desire for it, and, by which she intended, by and by, to turn the laugh against him. She took the egg, and breaking it, found it contained *more than she expected* and laid it quietly aside. Her husband could hardly refrain from laughing. This little "aside" occupied but a moment. To hide his merriment, he took up his knife and fork, and cut a piece of ham with a most resolute air, found he had, at the same time, dissected a nicely-fried cockroach! A glance at Mary's face upset his gravity (his appetite had gone before), and rising hastily, he made some excuse about *caring for his horse*, and Mary rose a moment after to *attend to her baby*. But Mr. Herbert will be careful how he tells his wife again, that he never saw the table where he could not glean a meal!

When he returned, Mary was beginning to feel uneasy at his long tarry, but he informed her, that Charley had, against his express orders, been most improperly fed, and was very sick. The landlord and himself had been doing all that could be done, till morning, and he added:

"As the stage passed here two hours ago, and there is no other till day after to-morrow, we have the very delightful prospect of tarrying for at least two days, should the horse remain ill."

"But 'tis getting late, and we may as well retire to the 'imposing apartment,' here provided."

Imposing indeed! The whole of the upper story was before them, without a partition, and containing four exceedingly uninviting beds, one of them, to Mary's confusion, being occupied by two snoring Dutchmen, and the one nearest her own, by a woman and three children, the youngest using his lungs right lustily.

Mary told her husband he might venture to try the bed if he chose, but she was afraid of being devoured alive, or something worse, if she tried to rest on such vile-looking affairs. Mr. Herbert determined to risk the trial; and taking a clean towel from her travelling-basket, his wife pinned it around the brown and stained pillow, and spread the buffalo robe on the floor for her babe, covering him with her shawl. Then drawing a chair near the baby, she seated herself with her feet on the rounds, and her dress carefully gathered off from the floor, preferring to pass the night as a watcher.

It was but a short time after all the arrangements had been made, when both father and child, who, from fatigue, had quickly fallen asleep, became very restless; she lighted a bit of candle, to ascertain the cause. Oh horrors!—the wild beasts were abroad! The poor babe was in a sad condition, and on going to her husband's bedside, she saw a long, black procession, slowly moving from his arm, across his breast, and up the sides of his face.

"Wake up! wake up, George, or there will be nothing of you or the boy left by morning."

"Well, this *is* a little more than ever *I* can endure. If Charley can stand, only on three legs, I will not wait for daylight. I think we can't be more uncomfortable should we land in a mud-hole between here and Anderson's (the next tavern). So make yourself and that little martyr as comfortable as you can, while I go and take counsel of the horse.

In a very short time Mary heard Charley's step at the door, and needed no urging to hasten out.

The poor landlord was with Mr. Herbert. "I am very sorry you found such uncomfortable quarters; but, indeed, what can a poor man do?" said he, sighing.

It was sad, and they really wished, for his sake, they could have endured till morning. But, saying a few kind, comforting words to him, they rode away.

It was about three in the morning when they started, and for the first two hours they were obliged to move with great caution, both for want of light, and also because Charley was in no mood for fast labor. But as daylight slowly dawned around them, and their path became less obscure, even the horse, gathering courage, stepped briskly forward, and it was not long before they reached the next "bit of clearing." The "*house*" was but a one-story log cabin, and Mary thought the prospects not much brighter than before, judging from the exterior.

"Don't judge by appearances, my dear. The two-story house that excited your admiration when we first came in sight of it, did not serve us any too well; but I suspect, from what I have been told, that this will prove quite a godsend."

A surprise awaited them at the very door. On each side of the clean, wooden steps, was a little bed of marigolds, pansies, and pinks. Morning-glories and creepers shaded the windows, and a climbing rose formed a beautiful ornament for the rough log "stoop."

This simple evidence of a love for flowers won Mr. Herbert's heart.

"I know that we shall find something to eat that will be at least clean at this house," he said, "for no one that loves flowers can be a slattern."

The stout, tidy, motherly Dutch woman, who met them as they entered, smiled kindly when she heard the remark, and stepping to an adjoining shed, she requested her husband to aid her in hastening the breakfast for their weary guests. As she returned to the pleasant room, she said: "John and I don't keep 'help,' we love so much better to work together. He'll see to your horse presently, if you will be so good as to hitch him, till he has brought me some wood and water."

And truly it was a pleasant sight for our friends, to watch the loving old couple as they passed and repassed each other, and always with a smile, or pleasant word.

"What do you think my wife has been saying, my good dame?" said Mr. Herbert in his sportive way, while she was arranging the table. "She is wondering if we shall be as happy and fond of each other, as you and your husband seem to be, when we are as old. I tell her it will depend upon herself. If she is as gentle and good-natured as you are, I can't well fail of making a good husband. Is is not so?"

"Oh, no; I cannot agree with you, sir. If it had all depended on *me*, we should have been a very unhappy couple now, I dare say. I was very affectionate naturally, but irritable; and in the early part of our life, while my children were coming up around us, I had a great deal of hard work, and much pain and ill health, which did not make me gentle. But John always said, so long as he hadn't the pain and weakness to bear, no matter how hard he worked, he ought to be patient and kind with me, and I have never had a hard word from him yet, God bless him, though I'm 'shamed to say, I've given him a good many. He's always been ready to excuse my short-comings, and some of the time they have not been easy to bear, I assure you. I used to grieve over it, and think he'd get tired out with me, and not always be able to realize that it was labor and pain, and not my heart that made me ugly, and sometimes I longed to die. But he bore on, and now he has his reward, for a happier couple never did live, I know. My health, as my children grew up, improved, and I don't see now, but I am as good-natured as other people.

"No, no, you must allow me to differ from you, sir. I think my John is right. Men can have no idea of what a woman's feebleness and sufferings may be—the hundred weary days and nights of irritating pains, which take the courage and gentleness all out of one; and unless they are certain they could be more patient under the rod than their poor wives, they'd better in early married life be loving and gentle, and then they'll be sure of a peaceful old age. If John had judged me harshly *then*, I should have been ruined body and soul, and he would be wretched *now*.

"Well, now I've talked till I have kept your breakfast back; but I never know when to stop when I begin to speak of John."

"I'm sure I am very much obliged to you," said Mary, smiling, "and my husband looks as if he could not gainsay your remarks."

A broiled chicken and some hot venison steaks, were now smoking on the table, and added to these, some fine fresh tomatoes, potatoes, white as snow-balls, sweet bread, yellow butter, a dish of berries, with a pitcher of rich milk beside them; and, Mr. Herbert said, the best coffee he had ever tasted in a public-house!

The kind old man begged the privilege of holding the baby, while his wife waited on their guests.

"And surely," said Mary, "food never did taste half so good before. It is worth one's while to fast for a few hours, for the sake of such an appetite."

While partaking of their carefully prepared breakfast, they enjoyed a good deal of pleasant conversation with their host and his wife, and learned much of their earlier life, which interested them exceedingly, and the old couple appeared also much pleased with their society.

They belonged, it seemed, to a *good family* in Germany, and had received advantages far above what their present position would indicate.

It was a genuine *love-match*, with the usual amount of opposition, and producing the usual results. That is, it confirmed their love, and strengthened their determination to be united, at all hazards. They were married, and to escape strife and bitter words from his friends, who had wished him to choose a bride from a higher station, they left home and native land, and with a scanty pittance came to the new world, where, by hard labor and close calculation, they worked their way up to a pleasant competence, educated six sons and daughters, had seen them all well settled in life, and were now peacefully, hand in hand, going down into the vale together, their youthful love brightened and strengthened by toiling and suffering with, and *for* each other.

They could, if they had chosen, have built themselves a handsome home—but with the romance which is generally supposed to be the exclusive property of *youth*—the neat log cabin which their own hands had helped to build—beautified with the vines which, for years, they had together taught to twine about it, the thrifty shrubs and trees, each planted to mark the birth of a loved child, or commemorate some joy or sorrow shared together—and all the little conveniences which thoughtful affection had invented, or supplied, were dearer to those *old lovers* than the most splendid edifice in the land.

Our travellers had become deeply interested in the narrative which the old people had given, and felt reluctant to leave; and the interest seemed equally shared by their new friends, who urged them to spend the day, and rest. But George was to preach for his brother that evening, and it was full time they were on their way.

Their horse had been well cared for, and apparently entirely recovered, the guests most happily refreshed, and with many kind words and hearty thanks (for these good people would take no other remuneration, when they learned that Mr. Herbert was a clergyman), they bade them farewell, and were once more on their way.

CHAPTER XVI.

THE VISIT AND RETURN.

They found their brother and his wife in a commodious house, delightfully located, and surrounded with all the comforts and luxuries of wealth.

Sister Kate had lost her first child—a beautiful girl, about the age of little Susie—but she had a baby *George* to show, a fine little fellow of two years.

The first evening, they returned from the church at an early hour, being greatly fatigued; but when seated once more with those dear ones, there was so much to enjoy, so many things to recall and talk over, that they forgot entirely the last restless night, and were in danger of being sleepless from pleasure, as they had then been from discomfort.

"Do you remember that visit to Oakley, Sister Mary, when you came to arrange for your first attempt at housekeeping? And, do you know, I thought you must be entirely ignorant of money matters, or household expenses, when you were so sure you could contrive a comfortable home for this good brother with such materials as you were able to collect? I felt sad when we parted from you that morning at the wharf; for I was so sure you would find your plans a failure."

"Very likely, I should, had it not been for the kindness of friends; and if I had had also the benefit of my present experience, the prospect would have been a dark one, indeed. We have seen harder times than those, however, when closer economy was necessary; and yet, somehow, we have never been so closely hedged in, but there has been some way of escape provided, and often when our courage has been well-nigh exhausted; and I presume, we shall continue to find it so."

"Well," said Frank, "riches can never make a pleasanter home than those two rooms in Glenville, and we shall never spend happier weeks than we spent there, I'm sure."

"I often envy you," said Kate, "the pleasure of being *compelled* to manage and contrive all possible ways to get along. Still more, the ability to do so, and yet keep a bright home for your husband, under every discouragement. I wonder if I *could* do it. I think I should like to try."

"It does very well to dream over and long for, when seated as we are now, with everything comfortable and elegant about us," said George; "but my poor wife's faded roses, and the silver in her curls, after only six years of such contrivance, show you that there is something more serious than romance about it."

"True, and these late hours won't recall the roses."

"Ah! now. Let me tell you," replied Mary, "'tis not short pay or hard work that have blanched my cheeks or silvered my hair, but those abominable chills you force upon the stranger within your gates in this western world. I'm certain I could work as hard as I have done, and calculate as closely, and contrive as ingeniously, and yet be quite a young lady, when fifty years old, if our field of labor was in a more healthy location. It is this shaking business that destroys the wives and mothers."

An exceedingly happy week passed by. The labors and preaching of the two clergymen were greatly blessed to the people, and endeared the brothers and sisters, still more closely, to each other. After their return from the nightly meetings, they would sit conversing till the small hours, feeling that the pleasure of such intercourse was worth more to them than sleep.

But, pleasantly as passed the hours, the mother, at the end of two weeks, began to long for her children. She well knew that Susie's loving heart was counting the hours passed away from her parents, and little prattling Frank would long for his father's good-night frolic, and his mother to prepare him for his crib; and so, with the promise of an early visit from their brother and sister, they separated.

In returning, they took another and more pleasant route home, and found very comfortable accommodations on the way, but none that had the charm for them of that one-story log tavern, with its simple-hearted, loving occupants.

When they reached home, little quiet Susie sprang into their arms, and wept and sobbed till her parents were alarmed for the effects of such nervous excitement; while Master Frank jumped and laughed in true boy's style, and wondered why sister cried when pa and ma came home. Cousin Helen, also, was quite willing to resign her honors, saying she found it much easier to be taught, than to practise what she had learned.

Mr. Francis called in the evening, and received the hearty thanks of both Mr. and Mrs. Herbert, for the pleasure of their journey; the latter saying she felt almost as strong as before her illness, and sure that nothing but her release from care, and the delightful visit to their friends, could have done her half so much good.

"Then, I presume," said Mr. Francis, with a smile, "you will no longer need Helen, and are quite prepared to commit her to my keeping?"

"That's wicked and unkind! to use our thanks for your generosity as weapons against us. I think it no more than fair, after that, to keep her another year. It will seem too much like a *bargain*, now, sir. *My wife's journey* for *our cousin Nellie.* I wouldn't have a word to say to such a mercenary man, Nellie!"

"Ah! I am beforehand with you. I have her promise, that if Mrs. Herbert returned quite recruited, she would not refuse to take charge of me very soon. You need not have expended such an amount of gratitude for the trifling service I rendered you. Don't you see, it was all sheer selfishness?"

"No such thing," said Mary; "you can never make us believe your slanders on yourself, Mr. Francis. It is just like you, to try and make people imagine you worse than you really are."

"You think that's bad enough, without any effort to increase the dark shades. Do you not?"

"You are an odd genius, Francis. I've known you take more pains to impress people with the idea that you are mean and selfish, than most persons would to secure the reputation of saintship. But you can't fool my wife or me. I understand you well. If I had not, you should never have secured a claim on our blushing cousin here. Nellie, you have your life's work before you, to keep this man in anything like order."

"To be sure she has; and, therefore, the sooner she begins, the more perfectly will her work be accomplished."

"You have the advantage of us again, and therefore we shall be obliged to leave Nellie to settle the question in accordance with her own judgment."

It was decided that the wedding should take

place at the end of the month. Mr. Francis had built and furnished a pleasant house, within a few steps of the parsonage, and Helen would hardly feel that they were not still one family.

Some weeks after the wedding, Mrs. Herbert told her husband that there seemed no way of getting through the year, but by taking boarders again; unless he thought it right to make a plain statement of their case to their principal men, and leave it with them to decide which was most for their interest, to pay at least the amount promised, or relinquish him to some church who would consider him worthy of a comfortable support. There were, already, she added, three hundred dollars due from their last year's salary, of which they had not been able to collect a penny, beside that which was unpaid on the present year.

"Just about as much due at the end of the year, as we gained by that donation party. How it would have grieved our dear Mrs. Jackson and Mrs. Tompkins, had they lived to see that their loving efforts, instead of shaming our business men into a more honorable course, has acted as an opiate to their consciences, and we have been more sorely pinched than ever before."

"Well, dear, what shall we do? We have trusted their promises long enough—lived on the hope of '*better times*,' till we can live so no longer. Our garden and cow are indeed great helps to us, as far as food is concerned; but the general wardrobe needs replenishing sadly, and additions to yours *cannot* be any longer deferred. I have mended your coat and vest, till it will hardly hold the stitches, and breaks out by each day's wear, so that I am compelled to sit up and mend at night, after you retire. Last Sabbath, you know (after I had mended Saturday night as near to twelve as I dared), you burst out the sleeves, just writing your sermon, and I was obliged to take my needle and mend till the last bell rang. I had a great mind to send you to preach without a coat."

"I think it might have been a good plan," said her husband, smiling. "I would have said, on entering the pulpit, 'The brethren and sisters must excuse my unclerical appearance, but my *only* coat would not hold fast its integrity until after preaching, and my wife's conscience will not allow her to mend it on the Sabbath. My people will not pay me for my labor, and I cannot, therefore, buy a new one.' Don't you believe such a speech would rouse them to a sense of their shortcomings?"

"Doubtful. I told Brother Hudson (who boarded with us, you know, when we first came here) about my being obliged to mend your coat, before you could go to church, a few weeks since, and would you believe it, he was fired with righteous indignation at my presumption in thus desecrating the Sabbath.

"'Why,' said I, 'you would not have your pastor preach with a coat-sleeve hanging only by a seam, would you?'

"'Couldn't he put on his second-best coat, just for once, rather than have you sewing on the holy Sabbath?'

"'Certainly, sir, if he *had a second-best*, a convenience (or *luxury* perhaps you would call it), which he has not been able to afford for years.'"

"That was rather a *poser*, was it not?"

"Only for a moment, for he soon replied:

"'Well, I must say, Mrs. Herbert, if you would economize more closely (! !) you might manage to keep our minister more respectably clad.'

"'*As for instance*'— said I.

"'Well—well.—Oh, many things.'

"'Too vague altogether, Mr. Hudson. You must particularize if you wish me to profit by your remarks.'

"'Well, your table. I remember I used to think, when in your family, that you lived far more expensively than was necessary—pies or puddings every day, etc.'

"'Why didn't *you* suggest this *while with us?* If my memory does not fail me, you seldom objected to my replenishing your plate the second time, and of course I took that as a sign of your approval.'

"Just then he remembered a business engagement, and was obliged to leave suddenly. I expect you will lecture me for speaking so plainly, but how could I help it?"

"Not very easily, my dear; and you may be sure I shall not trouble you with a lecture. I imagine he only got his *deserts.*

"But what to do about our affairs I don't know. I have little hope that they will improve while we stay here. Our people, I think, feel that, should it come to the trial, we could not find it in our hearts to leave them; and, as we have managed to keep along thus far, they think we always can. I can't en dure the thought of leaving, but I fear it must come to that."

"It seems so unaccountable that a church should ever be inclined to grudge a minister a tolerable support. Their health or pockets would suffer if the lawyer or physician were treated as carelessly, but their free and easy habits have not taught them to place any great value on the services of one who labors for their souls' well being."

"I would go to Mr. Francis for advice, but that would be just the same as asking him to put his hand into his purse and give me a bank bill."

"Oh, no; it will not do to go to him. But why not have a long, plain talk with Father Tompkins?"

"Is it possible I did not tell you that he was struck with paralysis last night, and is helpless and speechless to-day? How could I be so forgetful!"

"Dear old man! The cords that bind us here are dropping asunder, one by one. Perhaps it is the only way to decide us to leave. But the sweetness of their memory will ever make the place dear. We had better lay aside our own affairs, and go over and see if we can be of any service to him, or his family."

Mr. Tompkins lived only a few days, uncon

scious all the time, and then passed from earth to join his companion in heaven. He had been steadily failing from the day of her death, but never was a man better prepared for a change of worlds. He had long before put his house in order, and lived as if he felt each day might be his last.

The two eldest daughters had married since their mother's death. The sons had commenced business in a neighboring town, and now the youngest daughter went to find a home with her sisters, and our friends' connection with this family was entirely broken up.

But now the pastor's private affairs would no longer admit of delay. The crisis had come, but how to meet it in the kindest spirit, and with the requisite firmness, was the question.

Mr. Jackson, since his wife's death, had been considerably disturbed, and embarrassed in his own business matters, and it was thought doubtful if his mind could be brought to look into the subject under consideration, so clearly, as to make it advisable for him to attempt any change, for them, either by private conversation, or a more formal presentation of their case to the people. Mr. Herbert, therefore, decided to assume the responsibility of calling his principal business men together, and plainly show them the true state of his finances, and insist upon a reformation, or dismissal from his charge. But just before the evening appointed for this painful task, he received a letter from Mobile, inviting him to take charge of a church in that city, and offering him a very liberal salary, beside paying his debts (if he had any) and defraying the expenses of removing his family to the place.

"This is bringing matters to a crisis, suddenly," said he, after reading the letter.

"Why, George, you haven't *decided* to go?"

"No, indeed. I shall say nothing of it, till I have carefully thought over the whole ground, on both sides. My present feeling, however, is, that it will be best to lay this letter before our people, as *a body*, and if they *really* wish me to remain, tell them a prompt and decent support are the only conditions on which I can stay. If they rouse up and act effectively, I think I can do more good here than in Mobile. But if, as I have of late more than once thought, they have withheld our support, hoping I should ask a dismission, the way they receive this letter will settle the doubt beyond a question."

"Why, my dear husband, you can't be serious in supposing there is any dissatisfaction with you. The idea never entered my mind."

"No, my dear, I suppose not; because it is a *wife's mind*, and no such ideas could possibly creep in there. I did not suppose *you* were dissatisfied, love. But others may not see with your eyes, or appreciate your husband's efforts quite as highly as you do. However, a few days will settle the question. We will not speak of it again, for the present."

At the close of the week, Mr. Herbert told his wife that he had decided to inform his people, on the next Sabbath, of the call, and appoint a general meeting, for the Tuesday following, to take the question into careful consideration.

The eventful Tuesday brought a very full attendance, and the reading of the call produced great excitement. Few could realize that *such* an offer could be declined. But immediately after the communication, Mr. Herbert said he wished, before any action was taken upon it, to make a frank, and very plain statement.

He then calmly reviewed the last seven years, distinctly stating how very severely they had been straitened, how seriously his wife's health had been injured, by her efforts to supply *their* deficiencies, and concluded by informing them that the feeling had for some time been growing upon him, that nothing but a reluctance on their part to support him, and a desire for his removal, could have induced them to compel him, so long, to contend with difficulties which they could have so easily removed. He would, therefore, now withdraw, and leave them unembarrassed by his presence, to settle in their own minds, what answer *they* would wish returned to the people of Mobile.

The next morning, a committee called at the parsonage, bearing the results of their deliberations.

They had examined into their accounts, and were surprised and ashamed to find themselves largely in their pastor's debt. The deficiency had been collected on the spot, and a vote taken to raise the salary two hundred dollars, and a committee appointed to see that it was paid promptly every quarter.

"The vote was unanimous," said the committee,

'save one dissenting voice, and that you will be surprised to learn was your cousin's husband, Mr. Francis."

"Some of his eccentricity, I presume. But what reason did he give?"

"'Oh, it costs a good deal to keep a man like Mr. Herbert, and he guessed we'd better hunt up a cheaper preacher.' We could not persuade him to pay a cent toward making up the arrears. That's a specimen of his pretended friendship for you, I suppose."

"Oh, I'll risk Francis' friendship. It will all be explained to my entire satisfaction, and his complete vindication from anything more than oddity, I am confident."

"Well, we hope you'll give us the benefit of his reasons, when you find them."

"Very likely the only way I shall ever get at them, will be by a promise to leave you all as much in the dark as you now are."

"It is strange—no matter what he does, you appear to think Francis always right."

"Not exactly *right*, for I don't believe in cheating people into forming false estimates of any one. But he is a right noble, generous fellow, with all his faults, as we have tested in more ways than we can speak of."

"Well, let that pass. Will you now dismiss this call, Mr. Herbert, that has given us all such a start?"

"Certainly, if the *start* produces *permanent* effects. I am greatly attached to this people, and beside, honestly think I can do more good here than in a new place, if you perform your duty by a strict observance of the promises voluntarily made. But I warn you fairly, I will never be brought to this strait again, and remain with you. I can't afford to be constantly '*bickering*' with my people about money matters, nor can I see my wife go down to a premature grave from needlessly hard work."

That same evening, Mr. Francis and Nellie came in for a social chat. Mr. and Mrs. Herbert had resolved to make no allusion either to the call or the decision of the people. It was evident he was all impatience to open the matter, and learn their opinion of his procedure. The evening was far spent, and no mention had been made of the call, or anything connected with it; but as they rose to leave, Mr. Francis said:

"I suppose you are angry that I advised your accepting that call."

"Oh, no, not at all angry. But let's have your reasons for wishing me to leave, and I'll promise to go to-morrow, if *you* really think I ought."

"Well, if I choose, I could give most excellent reasons, and if I did, would surely hold you to your promise, to go immediately. But then I'm *timid*, and dislike to talk contrary to the public voice. They might mob me, or burn my store if I did."

He then handed Mr. Herbert a check for fifty dollars, saying, "I wouldn't give you a cent, only Helen quarrelled with me so for not subscribing at the meeting, that, for peace sake, I came this evening to give you this."

"It is not true, Cousin George, indeed it is not! He said he wouldn't give at the meeting, because they had been so mean in allowing your salary to remain so long unpaid, and as he has always paid prompt himself, was not going to help them out of a ditch of their own digging. Beside, he said, now they were frightened, they would have no trouble in raising it without his help, and this which he has handed would be clear gain."

"Do just talk to him, cousin, and tell him it is wicked to try to make people think so wrongly of him."

"Tell *her* it is wicked to betray her husband's confidence in this way."

And they said good night with happy hearts—leaving happy ones behind them.

"Oh, 'tis such a relief," said Mary, when alone with her husband, "to know that we shall not be obliged to leave! They have done better than I expected, in paying up all arrearages, and it will enable us to start free from debts once more. But do you feel confident they will keep these promises better than their first?"

"Very doubtful. But 'sufficient unto the day is the evil thereof.' We will trust them till they compel us to doubt, and then, they have been fully warned, and can blame no one but themselves, if the consequences of their folly prove disagreeable."

CHAPTER XVII.

THE TRUE SPHERE OF WOMAN.

MRS. HERBERT had not thought it advisable to increase her labors by receiving any boarders, as the promised addition to their income, and the payment of that which had so long been due, would, she hoped, cancel all their bills, and enable them to pass the year, upon which they were now entering, less anxiously than heretofore. Indeed, without any servant, the regular work of her own house, the care of her three little ones, and all the family sewing, unaided by a "Wheeler & Wilson," or a "Grover & Baker," and a large amount of company, would appear to most of our readers quite as much as one pair of hands could be expected to perform. But to Mrs. Herbert this was luxury compared to some of the past years, for though few meals, if any, passed without a guest at their table, this seldom interfered with the enjoyment of their evenings. These, with the exception of the regular weekly meetings, were always spent together, and there would be an hour or two, even after the meeting, when, her children quietly sleeping near, and her husband, with book or pen at the same table where she sat busy with her needle, eager to listen to any chance remark, or a sentence from his writing, she thought that no one could ever have been so happy as herself.

Their garden, also, was a great source of healthful enjoyment, as well as a very necessary part of their support.

Mary was an early riser, and her husband had long since confessed that he could never have accomplished so much but for this habit. Their breakfast was over, and the morning's work all finished before their neighbors were stirring, and then, if Mr. Herbert had no early engagement, they took the little ones to the garden, which was some distance from the house. Spreading an old rug or blanket on the grass, little Susie was left to care for Frank and Harry, while their parents were at work; Mr. H. taking the rougher part, left the transplanting and "clearing up" to his wife. These were the bright, happy hours, compensating for the pain and toil of many dark ones.

Their garden was an uncommonly fine one, yielding an abundant supply of choice things, aside from what they gained by sending a large quantity of vegetables into market. They could boast of the largest lettuce, the finest peas, the earliest corn and melons, and of the best and choicest variety.

Then the pears, peaches, and cherries—could any be found that tasted half so sweet or juicy as theirs? No market ever furnishes vegetables and fruits so palatable as those which our own hands have planted and gathered. Mr. and Mrs. Herbert well understood this, and often when wearied with care, or harassed and vexed by some sad development of human nature in those around them, they would say, that one hour's work together, in this pleasant spot, could dispel the clouds, and enable them to judge more charitably, or endure more patiently, the faults of others, besides making it far easier to correct their own.

Their little patch of ground abounded in valuable fruit-trees, most of which had been set out after weekly evening meetings, often late in the night, Mary holding the lantern and steadying the tree, while her husband placed the earth about it.

Happy hours! Toil and poverty could not take them from them, or, should brighter days dawn in after time, and under more prosperous circumstances, will not their hearts turn from affluence and the highest refinements of life, with intense longings for the simple joys shared *together*, and enriched by pleasant and affectionate converse!

Mr. Herbert's great pride was in his flower garden, and indeed it was shared by half the place. When he first settled in Norton, ornamental gardening was hardly known, except in very rare cases. The good people would have thought it very ridiculous to have been found busy over a *flower-bed.* It was too childish, and besides, "What's the *use?* What good will they do?" "What good! why, they make you happier and better every time you look at them. Try it a year, and you will never ask that question again." And their minister determined that they should cultivate a taste for the bright and beautiful flowers.

He began their course of education, by being almost always seen with a rose or rare flower in his hand, which he gave, in the course of his walks and calls, to such as appeared most likely to appreciate. It was given by "*our minister*," and that was, at first, its chief value. But flowers cannot be brought before any one constantly, without their learning to love them for themselves, as well as for the giver.

Sometimes, Mr. Herbert would put a choice rose in a pot and take it to an invalid, telling them to watch its growth and minister to its necessities, and it would take from a sick room half its tediousness.

Occasionally, during a call, he would speak of some beautiful plant that he had found in full bloom in his yard, that morning; and when, by his happy way of describing, he had gained the attention of the family, and created an interest, would point to a place in their own garden where the plant or shrub would look finely; and add, if it would be gratifying, he should be happy to transplant it there himself.

In this way, a floral interest had been gradually developed among the people, and at the time I write, few small cities could be found, where ornamental shrubs and trees were so abundant, or selected with greater taste.

"Time rolls its ceaseless course." Eight years have ploughed some deep furrows in the smooth brows, and sprinkled many a thread of silver in the brown locks, of our friends. On Mrs. Herbert life's burdens had left deeper traces than on her husband. She had not his healthful elasticity of spirit and natural mirthfulness, or hopeful way of looking upon life. She did not see the "silver lining" which was always visible, to his eyes, "through every cloud." An unusual amount of sickness and severe suffering had fallen to her lot; and added to that, a degree of physical labor far beyond her strength, and from which it was impossible for her husband to shield her, without a constant neglect of most important duties. There had been many hours, as she felt strength and capacity for exertion diminishing, when her youthful aspirations were brought vividly back to her mind; and the old longing for high intellectual attainments returned with giant strength. Then, contrasting her present life with her girlhood's plans and resolutions, her heart shrank back from the homely reality. To spend a lifetime in this weari some, unchanging routine—caring only for bodily wants—to cook—to wash and mend—was that all woman was born for? Was a wife who could do *only* that, a meet companion for the husband in whom she gloried? Would the fullness of her love, poured out so lavishly upon him, satisfy the wants and necessities of a mind like his? In her earlier married life, these periods of despondency had been a sad drawback to her happiness, though carefully hidden in her own heart; but they had yearly diminished, as her husband's unvarying gentleness and loving care taught her daily more and more confidence in her ability to make his home all-sufficient for his wishes. She was learning to place a higher estimate on purely domestic qualifications—to feel that a woman's proper ambition should be, the endeavor to relieve her husband, especially if a professional man, from those home-cares which are incompatible with high mental effort—that he may turn, when wearied and perplexed with parochial or public duties, to his own hearth as a *resting-place*—the sweetest earthly refuge for care and trouble. I am aware that the *strong minded* females of this progressive age will be exceedingly disgusted with such a sentiment; nevertheless, to a *true woman*, it *is* the sweetest, noblest mission that life can offer. It is, I am persuaded just what God meant woman to do. He has left the bolder, more exposed, and demonstrative paths in life for man, and bestowed on woman the privilege of shining with a softer light, sheltered and guarded by manly love, in a home made heavenlike by her graceful care and gentle influences. The woman, so happily endowed as instinctively to fill out the picture which rises before my mind, but which my pen so feebly portrays, need feel no envy at any *public* distinction or applause secured by some of the more ambitious but less favored of her sex.

Mrs. Herbert had succeeded better than the generality of wives in satisfying her husband, that his home was one of the best resting-places in the world, and now that her health was so rapidly failing, her chief sorrow arose from the fear that it would become so hopelessly impaired as to disable her from making this place any longer desirable; and the old longing for a higher state of mental culture, that she might still continue to be in some degree a meet companion for him, distressed her exceedingly.

There were also other sources of anxiety that could no longer be concealed. Two years had passed since the good people of Norton had been frightened into thoughtfulness by the call from Mobile, spoken of in the last chapter. For some months all went smoothly, but then their affairs began gradually to fall back into their old channel. Before one year was passed, they were again in debt to their pastor, but *promising* to bring all right the next quarter. The second year was now nearly ended, and their prospects were growing darker every month. The conviction was confirmed, that they must soon bring their minds to leave. This was of itself a painful thought, but darker clouds were gathering around them.

Mary was often cheered by pleasant messages from Hill Farm. Her father and mother, after a life of toil, were enjoying a happy and peaceful old age. The doctor's character became mellow and refined by advancing years, and his invaluable wife was reaping the fruits of her patience and gentleness in his ready acknowledgment of the aid she had been to him, and high estimate of her worth. Her children, scattered all over the land, rose up and called her blessed. Few had more of life's sweet ties and bright promises to make this world desirable, and yet very few lived more constantly prepared to resign her choicest treasures at her Father's call.

One morning, after an absence of a few hours, as Mr. Herbert entered his door, he was exceedingly alarmed by his wife's appearance. She sat by the window, with an open letter in her hand, and as he entered, a ghastly smile quivered on her lip. He hastened to her aid, and passing his arm fondly around her, bent over her and read one line. It was enough. "My poor wife!" He pressed a fervent kiss upon her brow, and as he gathered her trembling form in his sheltering arms, her tears flowed freely, and the bewildered brain found relief. Dr. Leighton was dead! He had passed from his wife's presence with a playful word, and a smile on his lip, and was brought back to her, but a moment after, a corpse.

The intelligence had been abruptly communicated to his daughter at a time when she was least able to bear it, and that night she gave birth to a puny little girl, and was herself for many days in great danger. It was the first death that had occurred in her father's family—the first broken link in the chain that had been growing brighter for forty years.

Who was to be the next? It made life and all its ties very uncertain, more so than any trial of her past life. It was many weeks before she could in any degree rise above the stunning effects of the shock. Her health continued very frail, and her babe did not thrive as her children had usually done. Some rest from home cares appeared absolutely necessary.

In this emergency, Mr. Francis and her cousin again came to the rescue. Mr. Herbert was obliged to cross the prairies to attend some convention, which journey he had designed to take on horseback, as the least expensive mode of conveyance. But Helen's whole-hearted husband offered them a carriage, and again handed Mrs. Herbert the money, for all needful expenditures for themselves and children; their church meanwhile looked on, and saw these arrangements to prolong her existence effected by *charity*, while they were in her husband's debt nearly four hundred dollars of the last two years' salary. But Mr. and Mrs. Herbert knew it was no fault of their own, that they were placed in circumstances which made it absolutely necessary that they should accept this gratuitous assistance, and therefore did not allow pride to prevent their receiving it as gratefully, as it was freely offered.

This journey was a new era in their life's history —a glorious spot of sunshine, following a dark and gloomy storm. Prairie travelling was a novelty to both. Broad plains, eighteen and twenty miles in extent, without a tree, shrub, fence, or building. Even the road, traceable often only by an occasional deep "slew hole," where some unfortunate teamster or traveller had been "*stalled*," and broken up the earth around in his efforts to extricate himself and team from his uncomfortable position. Passing those way-marks, they would ride miles, guided by the sun, through nature's flower-gardens, regularly laid out in broad strips, or patches, with colors tastefully blended, harmonized, or contrasted. Acres of wild roses, in full bloom, joined by equally extensive fields of purple, red, or crimson zenias; then the large, white oxeye, the golden buttercup or coryopsis, and the deeper purple, almost black iron-weed—the only dividing line between being the change in color, as one species of flower abruptly displaced the other. The scene was varied occasionally by a flight of birds, or a troop of deer, startled by their approach, bounded swiftly across their track, and were soon lost to sight in the tall grass beyond. Silence reigned all about then, broken only by their own voices, or the slight sound of their horses' feet, on the soft, green sward.

The monotony of prairie travelling soon becomes almost painful, and our travellers learned to hail the strips of woodland, or clearings, as they are called, which occurred every fifteen or twenty miles, with the pleasure one meets an old friend, after a sojourn among strangers.

These clearings, the only inhabited spots they passed for two days, consisted of a tavern, store, and sometimes a post-office combined, a rude church, and two or three log-houses; and here, where they stopped to rest and refresh themselves and horses, the accommodations closely resembled those described in another chapter. But every moment was too full of happiness and pleasure to be disturbed by any trifling discomforts; besides, experience had taught them many contrivances for overcoming the inconveniences and annoyances of western travelling.

Their children were all with them, and nothing left at home to cause anxiety. Two weeks flew by, full of unmixed enjoyment, and, refreshed in body and mind, and with spirits more elastic than they had been since Dr. Leighton's death, they turned their faces homeward, cheerful and happy.

But before they had alighted from the carriage, they were met on the very threshold of home with tidings of the most afflicting nature. Their beloved brother Frank, surrounded by all that makes life desirable, free from many of the cares and trials which had fallen to his brother's lot, with a wide field of labor spread out before him, and a heart zealously devoted to his work, had, thus early in life, fought the fight, finished the work allotted him, and gone home to his God and Saviour, leaving a desolate home, a mourning people, and a host of aching hearts—but the most entire confidence that their loss was his infinite gain. Oh! nobly had his work been done! and now he rests from his labors. Blessed spirit!

Little as their respective fields had allowed them to be together, to Mr. and Mrs. Herbert, their brother's death was one of the most severe afflictions that had ever befallen them—a loss that, even if they linger till old age, will never be forgotten—a vacant place in the heart's treasure house which can never be refilled.

CHAPTER XVIII.

DEATH OF LITTLE HARRY.

About this period, a brother, next younger than Mrs. Herbert, came to reside in Norton, bringing with him a wife and two little boys, whom she had never seen. He had, for some years, been settled in one of the southern cities, and had married there.

No event could have given our friends greater pleasure or comfort at this time, while their hearts were so saddened by the death of Mr. Herbert's brother.

Young Dr. Leighton had been almost as a twin-brother to Mary, during her girlhood, and was especially dear to her husband. He was the recipient of all her youthful trials, and enjoyments—the trusty friend and sympathizing adviser, during the troubled period of her long and eventful engagement, and though he had left home and entered into business before her marriage, they had always corresponded regularly; but since her wedding-day had met but once. For some weeks they were all one family, and when his business arrangements for a permanent residence in the place, were completed, they were still almost within speaking distance. The two families, together with their cousins, formed a delightful little circle, and the interchange of visits recalled the pleasant days they had so sadly missed, since the death of Mrs. Tompkins, and Mrs. Jackson. In her brother's wife, she found just the companion her heart coveted. Good, sound sense, an excellently cultivated mind, and withal very affectionate and gentle-hearted.

With such added ties to bind them to their people, who, though so regardless of their interest and comfort, were still truly beloved, the prospect of being absolutely compelled to abandon the field, by their neglect and carelessness, was more than ever distressing, and they were encouraged by Mr. Francis and Charles Leighton, to risk the accumu lation of debts, and make another year's trial; the two gentlemen taking good care the church should understand that it was through their advice, and not from forgetfulness on their pastor's part, of the failure of all their promises, as a people.

This year, which was to settle the perpetually recurring question, of the possibility of their remaining longer in Norton, was speeding onward. Soothed and encouraged, under all circumstances, by the presence of their brother and his wife, and constant intercourse with Mr. Francis' family, these few months were, in many respects, among their happiest days in Norton.

Little Susie was now almost eight, and her mother's ever-ready assistant; quiet and thoughtful, but capable and practicable beyond her years.

The rosy, little, five-year-old Frank, a bright and happy child, would gladly have contributed his mite of assistance in this industrious household; but, unfortunately, his love of mischief was perpetually overcoming his honest determination to make himself useful.

Little Harry was past three; a manly boy, and though merry-hearted and full of fun, he had less propensity for mischievous amusements, than his brother. As far as his distinguishing traits were developed, he manifested a closer resemblance to his father, than either of the children.

The babe had outgrown the sickly tendencies of

the first few months, and was now a curly-headed, beautiful little damsel, nearly two years old.

Their cousin's little one, of the same age, Charles Leighton's two sons, of seven and five, when united with the little circle in the weekly visits, interchanged between the three families, composed as beautiful a group as one could often meet. Few happier hearts could be found than the fond parents' when watching the merry gambols and roguish pranks of their beloved children.

But happiness, alas! is a transient guest, and the peace and quiet of these bright days were again disturbed by sickness and sorrow.

Little Susie, for the first time, bowed her fair head before the fever her poor mother had always so greatly dreaded, and from which herself and husband had so often suffered. It had been a source of deep thankfulness that their children had, so far, escaped, and now, to see their patient little daughter shivering in the chills, or tossing restlessly, in the paroxysm of fever, was a trial beyond expression bitter.

It is hard to witness sickness and suffering of any description, in old or young, especially when one feels powerless to relieve; but there are few things so painful to witness, as a young child *enduring* its first lesson in chills.

There is a strange mystery, which the little sufferer recognizes; a vague fear, which I have never seen manifested by a child in any other disease. The unnatural cold that creeps, creeps, creeps over the body, and then the terrible power that *will shake* the whole frame, in spite of the most resolute efforts to overcome it, is hard enough for older and stouter hearts to cope with; but a little child, with its tiny chilled fingers, its poor, blue, pinched nose, its anxious eyes turned, questioningly, from one attendant to another, will try a parent's nerves quite as severely as more acute suffering, or alarming illness can do.

Susie was taken suddenly one evening, and after a sleepless night, her mother had the satisfaction of seeing the darling child sink into a quiet slumber; both chill and fever having passed for the time.

Extinguishing her lamp as morning dawned, and giving one more sorrowful look at the exhausted little sleeper, Mrs. Herbert hastened to relieve her husband, who had risen, lighted the fire, and was now dressing, and trying to hush the two bright and merry boys.

Breakfast was over, the morning prayers had been offered, and as the children rose from their knees to receive the kiss always claimed at this time, Frank laid his head on his father's breast, saying, "I feel so sick, papa!" The blue lips, cold fingers and purple nails, told the nature of his illness, and he was immediately laid by his sister, a captive to the same stern tyrant. Judge how forlorn must have been the prospect, when the brightest spot that even Mr. Herbert, with his hopeful spirit, could see, was, "Well, my dear, it is a mercy that our poor little ones' chills will come on *alternate days*, and *one will be comparatively comfortable while the other is shaking*, and thus lighten, somewhat, your labor in nursing." And this was a comfort, the extent of which few of my readers can fully estimate, unless capable, by the power of imagination, of placing them in such circumstances as are here represented. No servants, two children sick, and two younger to be watched and guarded if possible from the same sufferings, and all, for sick or well, to be done by one person, and, after the first week, without the important aid her husband most kindly rendered. For, just at this period, it was important that he should be absent for two weeks, at a public meeting, and as the children were not dangerously ill, apparently, he was reluctant to decline going.

During his absence, Mrs. Herbert had every aid that her brother, Dr. Leighton, now fully established in Norton, could give; but both his wife and Mrs. Francis, who would have been invaluable assistants, were too ill themselves to assist; on the contrary, they were sources of painful solicitude to Mrs. Herbert themselves.

After a severe struggle, Susie and Frank began to convalesce, and when their father returned, had passed four days without a "chill," and could sit up a short time each day.

Harry, and little baby Nellie, met their father with shouts of rejoicing, and the two invalids, though pale and feeble, joined their voices in the loving "welcome home, papa." The dinner, that day, was prepared and eaten more cheerfully than before for many weeks. After tea, Mr. Herbert complained of fatigue and slight illness, which he thought a good night's sleep would remove, retired early, and Mrs. Herbert, whose only rest during the children's illness had been gained in a chair by their bedside, told her husband she must remain up a short time, to attend to some sewing, which sickness had accumulated, and would then try the luxury of retiring in a regular way.

Just then, her brother came in to make his call for the night. He examined the little sleepers, said all were doing well, and, as he himself had had a "chill" that afternoon, he would go home, and unless there should be some change for the worse, should not call the next day till late. Just as he left, he turned back and stooping to kiss little Harry, his especial favorite, said: "Sister Mary, Harry seems feverish, does he not? His pulse is quick, and his cheek too red. It is very slight, however, and may be but the heat of the room, though I don't quite like his looks. Don't be uneasy, but try to rest to-night yourself. If he should, by and by, grow restless, give him this powder." Mrs. Herbert stood watching the child, for some moments after her brother departed; but detecting no cause for alarm, sat down to her sewing till near midnight, then excessive weariness compelled her to prepare for rest. While at work, she had placed her chair where she could constantly watch little Harry's slumbers, and they were so gentle and undisturbed as to relieve her entirely of anxiety. But as she drew his little crib close to her bedside, she detected some strange change—she knew not what, save that it made her own heart beat wildly. He was deadly pale, and the perspiration stood in great beads on his brow. As she raised him in her arms, he moaned, then throwing himself back, his limbs stiffened in a fearful convulsion.

She called loudly for her husband, who was instantly by her side. Dressing hastily, he ran at once for her brother. When the two returned, the convulsion had passed, but the child lay unconscious in his poor mother's arms.

And so for eight long, sad days he lingered, fading, fading, still fading. The gently heaving breast alone gave token of life; not a moan, or effort at motion, disturbed the fearful quiet of that little form! Can this be rosy, bright and active Harry! He whom his mother had always held—half unconsciously to herself—a *little* closer than the others, *because* he was *papa's miniature*, and was going, some day, to be like him—a good and noble *man!* and fill his father's place in the world, when he was old and past labor. How often, in his baby days, had she softly murmured all this in those low tones with which fond mothers are wont to lull their treasures to rest! How often, as months sped by, carrying him from babyhood to boyhood—when, mother-like, before retiring, she gave a last look to each pretty sleeper—had she pressed her lips to Harry's noble brow, and whispered, "*Dear papa's own boy!*" Then feeling half guilty lest she had wronged the other dear ones, turned back to kiss them also. And when, fresh and rosy from the morning's bath, each happy, joyful birdling flew merrily to call the father from his garden-work, and Harry plead to be carried on his shoulder, "*because* he was papa's *own* little man," how had she smiled to think of the secret significance that expression had to her own heart!

The sun was spreading its morning's beauties over the earth—a bright beam stole into that sad, darkened room, and rested on the face once so beautiful and rounded, now—oh! how sunken and ghastly! Good old Charley, who for days had been sadly neglected, was just freed from the confinement of his stall, and trotted briskly up to the door for the morning greeting he had ever been accustomed to receive from the children.

Poor Charley! will you ever carry your little master so gently round the yard again, curbing your proud, fiery steps and yielding your great strength to the guidance of that tiny hand? Oh, what a spasm wrung the poor mother's heart, when, with a low *whinny* of disappointment, the true-hearted steed paced slowly away, and she turned from the window to bend in agony over her boy! Her youngest brother had but the day before arrived, and was standing by the crib. The child, for the first time since his illness, opened his eyes. "Mamma, papa!"

She snatched him to her breast—"*Quick*, quick! Johnny, call George! He will live! *our boy will live!* Brother Charles and Dr. Brown said, if we could only rouse him, all would be well. Quick, Johnny, *quick!*" There was no need, for the father heard that feeble voice, and already holds the boy close to his throbbing heart, while Johnny, seizing the halter, springs with one bound on Charley's back, without hat, saddle, or bridle.

It needs but a word to put the noble beast to his full speed. His fleet footsteps but ring and echo on the little bridge, ere horse and rider are lost to sight, and in a few moments Dr. Leigh ton and his partner were with them. Mr. Herbert still held the darling child; one little, pale hand is pressed to his father's cheek; the other, as when in health, thrown lovingly round his neck; while the mother, with tears of joy and hope bedewing her face, is kneeling at her husband's side. "Oh, brother, he woke and knew us all and played a moment so sweetly with George's face! but, poor little fellow, he is so weak that he soon grew tired and sleeps now." Her husband's eyes are fixed on her brother's, for there is a fearful look upon his face, hardly consistent with such happiness as they were, but a moment before, feeling; and as Mary observed the expression, she tremblingly exclaims, "Why don't you speak, brother? You and Dr. Brown both said, if we could wake him to consciousness, he would get well."

Twice her brother essayed to speak, but failed. Mr. Herbert placed the babe in his mother's arms; the veins stood out like cords on his brow—and his lips were deadly pale, as, laying a cold and clammy hand on Dr. L.'s arm, he said:

"Speak, dear brother! Tell me all! I can bear it. *What do you fear?*"

The doctor placed his arms about the poor father,

saying: "My dearest brother, *this is nature's last effort*—our little noble Harry *is dying*."

No other word was spoken. The smile—half fear, half hope—with which Mrs. Herbert had greeted her brother, remained frozen on her lip, as she still held her precious child, while with burning brain, but tearless eyes, her husband seated himself beside her, in the vain effort to prepare for the coming struggle. Alas! *who* was *ever* prepared for this?

John Leighton had turned the panting steed loose into the yard, and at this moment, with radiant face, entered the room, to join in the congratulations which he anticipated when he left, and stood for a moment spell-bound at the change he encountered—then drew near to witness, for the first time, the approach of death. Scarce a movement or word broke the awful silence. There was nothing now to do but watch that cherished one, whose life was so quietly passing away, and as the sun, which, in his morning brightness, seemed to bring "healing in his beams," sank slowly down beneath the horizon, little Harry's last breath fanned his mother's death-like cheek, and his beautiful spirit returned to its home in heaven.

Nellie, the youngest, had been sent to her cousin's, Mrs. Francis, and the invalid children (kept in another room with a careful friend), had been almost forgotten during the dark hours of this miserable day; but now the thought that they must be told of their brother's death, and the fear that the shock might harm them seriously, in their feeble condition, roused the afflicted parents from the stupor of grief.

Little Susie heard the tidings, and looked on the dear one she had so often nursed, with deep, silent and most unchildlike sorrow; but Frank, in uncontrollable anguish, threw himself on the floor beside his cold and lifeless playmate, exclaiming: "Oh! mamma, mamma, I won't love God any more! You said he was good, but it's no good to take our pet Harry away from us; and I can't love him any more—oh, never!"

"Little Harry," said his father, soothingly, "my dear child, is very happy now. He has gone to heaven—to Jesus—among the glorious angels who sing God's praises forever."

"Oh, papa!" cried the child, "God has plenty of little angels up there to sing praises. He could have spared us our darling brother, I know."

Has there been no such reproachful cry wrung from older and truly Christian hearts in the first hour of sorrow and bereavement? Who shall too severely censure, if the same thought was echoed from the wretched mother's bosom? Not so with her noble husband, however. With the simple faith of a little child, he recognized a father's hand, meekly he bowed his head, assured that "He doeth all things well," and said, "Thy will be done."

Two days after, his face shining with the glorious consolations which were shedding their healing balm over his spirit, Mr. Herbert stood by the coffin of his beloved child, surrounded by weeping friends and parishioners, and *himself* conducted the funeral services before committing the precious form to the earth. And when, most tenderly, he seated the drooping mother in the carriage, in which had been placed the little coffin, that hid their beloved boy from their eyes, his face was radiant with the peace which passeth understanding, and the words of comfort, softly whispered into her ear, enabled her to stand by his side at that open grave, and see the child, which had known no colder cradle than her loving breast, laid therein.

But who can hear that fearful sound—the heavy fall of the earth on the coffin's lid—unmoved? The groan which burst from Mr. Herbert's breast, as he turned with his suffering wife to the carriage, was no dishonor to his faith and hope, for his master wept over the grave of Lazarus, even while knowing that his own voice would soon command the silent occupant to come forth and awake to a new life.

CHAPTER XIX.

CONCLUSION.

How many of those who may read these pages will at once, as is most natural, picture to themselves our friends' return to their desolate home. And they will imagine the sad and heavy-hearted father, hardly capable of attending to the most pressing duties; the drooping mother, clad in sombre robes, weeping away the heavy hours, or lying exhausted on the sofa, too absorbed in sorrow to notice the efforts of her remaining children to attract her notice or claim her care; and the servants gliding noiselessly about the house, in their simple-hearted sympathy with their employers' sorrows.

Ah, these luxuries of grief are not for the poor or for the faithful. No mourning apparel—no darkened rooms—no luxuriant sofa—no obsequious attendants to obviate the necessity for household labor, and give the trembling frame a moment for repose.

On the contrary, Mr. and Mrs. Herbert go back to their silent abode to resume laborious duties, which had only, for a few hours, been intermitted, and to force back into the deepest recesses of their own hearts the ever-present consciousness of their loss—

> "To miss his small feet on the stair,
> To miss him at the morning prayer,
> To miss him *all day—everywhere.*"

All this sorrow must be battled with in silence, for other afflicted ones are in their midst. They may not falter and sink beneath personal griefs. They must look above to their Master for help to bear their own burdens, and strength to comfort other mourners.

Mrs. Francis, though feeble, had been at the parsonage at little Harry's funeral, but Mrs. Leighton was very ill. Her third child was born the very day that her favorite nephew died, and Mrs. Herbert returned from the burial only to find an urgent request for her to come at once to her brother's. She found Sarah very feeble, and her husband seriously alarmed. There was no severe pain, but total prostration of the system, and apparently no power to rally. Still, it was difficult to believe that life was drawing to a close, while conversing with her.

Her sick-room was the pleasantest spot in the house. She was always cheerful, always satisfied and contented, receiving with affectionate gratitude each token of care and attention, and only anxious to cause as little trouble as possible.

She was not aware, as yet, of the fears that distressed her friends; but all felt confident that her heart was stayed on God, and that the summons to pass through the dark valley and cross the flood, would find her "fearing no evil, for the rod and staff" of Almighty love, would comfort and strengthen her.

No suffering disturbed her tranquil spirit. The chastening rod was laid very lightly upon her. When inquiries were made, from day to day, as to her health, her reply was, "Oh, I should feel quite well if I were not so *tired;*" and she often sportively added to Mrs. Herbert, "Sister Mary, won't your brother get out of patience with such an indolent wife? It does seem so ridiculous that I should call myself ill, when I have so little pain. If you and my husband did not manifest such solicitude, and care for me so tenderly, I should sometimes be half afraid that you might by and by think I made no effort to get well. But you are both so kind—true brother and sister in spirit, as well as by natural ties. It tries me greatly, darling sister, that I can be no help or comfort to you since our dear little Harry left us."

"Do not say so, dearest Sarah. It is a great relief from my own thoughts to come to you as often as I can, and if I could see you improving even a little, I think I should be almost happy once more."

Sarah was slightly agitated when she replied:

"Don't you think I *am some* better? I have several times thought by your manner lately—Mary, dear, you surely do not think me dangerously ill?"

She gazed earnestly into her sister's face, and could not fail to read the fears which had for some days distressed all her friends. The invalid covered her face with her hand, and the tears slowly glided between her pale fingers. After a long silence, she looked up, and save that her eye was brighter, hardly any trace of agitation was visible.

"This is very unexpected and sudden, my kind

sister, yet you need not so long have concealed your anxiety from me. I know in whom I have believed, and though it is hard, very hard, to leave loving friends—my dear husband and those precious little ones—yet, God knows best, and he will give me strength to part with them, fully assured of meeting all that my heart so fondly clings to, in that home where there will be no sorrow, and 'where the inhabitants shall no more say I am sick.'"

She continued for some days with no sensible change, speaking freely of her condition (for after a long and solemn conversation with her husband, he was compelled to acknowledge to her that he could see no prospect of recovery), and as calmly expressing her wishes respecting her children, and all pertaining to them, as if she was only preparing for a journey. To the very last she was free from pain, and even the final *struggle* with the *Conqueror* was most mercifully spared her. The last morning of her earthly life, she had appeared as well as usual, and was sitting up, when she suddenly exclaimed, "*I am so tired!* Please, dear husband, help me to the bed." He did so, and placed her in a favorite position. She looked into his face, with her own loving smile, and folding her hands upon her breast, closed her eyes, as if dropping sweetly to sleep. But in an instant she started, exclaiming, "Charles, Charles, dear Charles!" and ceased to breathe.

And thus another link, from the golden chain of earthly love, was carried by this dear sister, to unite our sorrowing friends still more closely to the heavenly world, and the precious ones safely gathered there.

The bereaved husband, and motherless children, were taken at once to the parsonage. The little babe, of but a few weeks, tarried only long enough to make the desolate house still more lonely, when he took his departure for the better home, to which his mother had ascended.

Under these circumstances, it would seem only natural to suppose, that in the hour of such severe trials, the people comprising Mr. Herbert's church and congregation would rouse to a realizing sense of the claims their pastor had upon them, and relieve him, at least, from pecuniary anxiety. *Not so at all.* They had bustling manifestations of sympathy for the sick-room, instead of efficient service—and tears in floods for the coffin and the grave, and for those, who, resting from life's cares, in the full enjoyment of unmixed blessings, were no longer conscious of the interest manifested—but dry eyes, and, *at best*, careless, heedless hearts, for the less favored survivors, to whom an *efficient sympathy*, or even *common justice*, would have been an unspeakable comfort and relief.

But *tears*, without *works*, are cheap; they cost the givers nothing, and are always on hand; but they will not clothe the mourner, or keep the house warm, or pay the grocer, and many other common, homely kind of things, which will put themselves in a body's way even when the heart is heavy, and the home *too still!*

The second year of trial, which Mr. Francis and Dr. Leighton had urged Mr. Herbert to give his people, before finally resolving to resign, was fast passing away. And after the first few weeks of wakening, no change was visible in the Norton fashion of supporting the Gospel. They slept as soundly as ever, and, weakened by illness, and bereavement, the good couple were becoming almost indifferent as to the result. It was at this time that an incident occurred which cut them to the heart.

When little Harry died, his father requested one

of the officers of the church to take charge of all the funeral arrangements, and at the same time, most earnestly entreated that all the bills connected with the sad ceremony might be discharged at once, so that no *business* allusions should ever be made to them upon this painful subject. The church and society were, at this very time, indebted to their pastor full three hundred dollars, and one would suppose that a commission so sacred as this would not be forgotten or neglected.

Just at this period, Mr. Herbert fell severely ill, and for some days a few of his most intimate friends, among the officers of the church, as well as the physicians, were in almost constant attendance. The room where he lay served as study, parlor, bed room, and hall—the front door opening directly into it. One day, just as the paroxysm of fever was passing away, two of the elders of the church and Dr. Leighton, were standing near the bedside, when a man rode close to the door-steps, so as to be able to look full upon the bed, and in a coarse, boisterous voice, called out: "I say there! Two or three weeks ago, I *made the coffin and buried a young one from here*, and was told that I wasn't to come here for my pay, but it would be handed me by the man who engaged the work. Wall, I've asked for it, and *asked for it*, and h'ant got the pay; and I tell you more, this 'ere way of doing business ain't my fashion. I am poor. I want my money, and will have it!"

Mrs. Herbert hastened to the door at the first sound, and tried to check the torrent of words before her husband should understand the matter. But she could not succeed. He started up in bed, and casting a severe and reproachful glance upon Mr. Sanders, one of the gentlemen to whom he had intrusted this most sacred commission, inquired why a request, made under such solemn circumstances, had been neglected. *Forgetfulness* was the only plea to excuse that which had caused them so cruel an insult. This was one of the things which, though forgiven, was never forgotten, and never could be, and which did more toward weakening the bonds that bound them to Norton, than all their past experience united. It was a manifestation of such heartlessness, that Mr. Herbert was half ready to believe the severity with which his wife sometimes expressed her opinions of the constant neglect of their comfort and happiness, which had characterized all their transactions, was more justifiable than he had ever been willing to concede before. All his natural kindness of heart and readiness to throw a broad mantle of charitable excuses over the faults or mistakes of those with whom he was associated—all his true and earnest love for the people of his charge, could furnish no cloak for carelessness like this. The naked fact was brought before them in all its selfishness, and they were compelled to face it. The result could only be a painful conviction, that though their church might value their labors very highly, and love them truly, yet, they received this labor as a natural right, and felt under no obligation to return any equivalent for health destroyed, and labor bestowed in their service.

The past year had, for various reasons, been more expensive than any previous one, and Mr. Herbert's labor more poorly compensated. Bills had accumulated, which could remain unpaid no longer, and yet, how were they to procure the money to settle them, if they could not first obtain that which was so justly theirs, and for which they had so faithfully labored?

The time for prompt and decided action had come The evil they had so much dreaded, was now right in their path, and from it there was no way of escape. Any further attempt to trust to the promised support of their Norton friends, would only end in involving them so that they could not pay those who had trusted to their honor. If they broke the ties uniting them to this church *now*, although they must go out from among them penniless, yet they could feel that they left none behind who would pecuniarily suffer through them. They had had some little assistance from eastern friends at various times, and Mr. Herbert had prudently invested it in a garden, upon which he was building a small house. By the sale of these, they could cancel all indebtedness; and it might be, that a part of their salary, still due, would be paid.

There were no fears with regard to another settlement. They had remained in Norton for *love*, not money or necessity. No three months had elapsed without bringing most urgent invitations to remove to churches, whose habits were more prompt and liberal than in their present position. Mr. Herbert would have chosen to spend his life in western labor, but his wife's health was so broken by the climate and over-exertions united, that her physicians recommended an eastern field. He had

had several invitations to return East, and settle, and the very week that he was taken ill, had received a most urgent letter to that effect from a church in a young and flourishing city near to their native place. It had remained unanswered some time, and a second had followed it, more earnest than the first.

To this he now replied, stating that the health of his family, and other circumstances, made it probable, that he should be obliged to remove from his present location, but, declining to give a definite answer for some weeks. His strong affections clung to this home, and almost unconsciously to himself, there was an undefined hope still lingering, that *something*—it would be difficult to say what—might yet enable them to remain.

Then followed some of the good clergyman's most harassing and trying weeks. He was compelled to call his people once more together, and lay before them again, a statement of his pecuniary embarrassments, and assure them that he no longer felt that any arrangement could now be effected, by which it would be safe for himself, or honorable to others, for him to remain with them longer. Of course this made a great commotion,

Most liberal resolutions, and generous promises, were offered, as once before, but not now, as then, followed by an immediate settlement of salary yet unpaid.

Both Mr. Francis and Dr. Leighton, were exceedingly distressed at the prospect of their leaving them, though Dr. Leighton did not deny that his sister could no longer endure the climate and labor united; but felt that her health might be restored if she could have the means of living less laboriously—and he gave these views very fully at the church-meetings.

It was a painful thing for Mr. Herbert to think of withdrawing from this field on account of pecuniary considerations, merely. Day after day, he asked himself if they could not live even more closely than before—if it was not wrong for a servant of Him who for our sakes became poor, and had not where to lay his head, to leave that part of the vineyard to which his master seemed to have called him, for such motives as these. The question was answered for him, in a way that enabled him to see other and stronger reasons for leaving; and such as left his conscience entirely free from doubt.

Mrs. Herbert was again attacked with sudden and alarming illness. When, at last, the immediate danger had passed, it left her system in a state that compelled an entire change of climate, as the only hope of final recovery. Thus, Mr. Herbert saw his course marked out for him, and had no hesitation in deciding to accept this interpretation of his duty.

It would be some time before he could remove his wife with safety, and he employed this interval in trying to secure the right kind of a man to fill his place; but soon saw that as long as he still remained with them, the people could see nothing desirable in another.

Meanwhile, Francis and Leighton were not idle, but trying, by every means in their power, to secure the full payment of what was still due. There was no trouble in securing *promises*—that had always been easy, but the fulfillment was as usual in the future.

Mr. Herbert's little house and garden were bought by a dear friend, and Mr. Francis engaged that it should be made to settle all demands that could be found against the original owner.

The people did, at last, succeed in raising a part

of what was due their pastor, but not enough to enable him to move his family east, and therefore everything they had, but Mr. Herbert's small library, and their very meagre wardrobe, was sold at auction; and not till the arrangements were all made, and the sale notified, did their church really wake up to the *certainty* that their pastor was in earnest. Then, indeed, when it was too late, did they manifest a degree of sorrow, only equalled by their former lethargy. Every plea that could be imagined was brought forward, every offer made to induce Mr. Herbert to change his mind, and consent to remain. As the matter was now beyond discussion, his love for them was still too strong to allow of any reproaches. It would do no good, now, to tell them, that for years they had had the power to retain him on their own hands, and it was their indolence and inefficiency which had broken the bonds which bound them together. He knew that they loved him, but he also knew that their promises were written on the sand. No kindness or liberality could now restore his wife to health or strength while there. It was all too late for severity or rebuke, and his heart prompted him to speak only of his wife's health, and leave it with their consciences to tell them if there were not other very important reasons back of that, and which were also the cause of her illness, that had really sent him from among them.

Mrs. Herbert's first effort was to write home; and we close with the letter to her mother:

"NORTON, *Dec.* —, 18—.

"MY DEAREST MOTHER:

"Your last letter has remained too long unanswered, but I have two very good reasons, which I know will free me from any appearance of neglect. First, I have been very ill, and for many days doubted if I should recover; and secondly, we have for some time felt the necessity of changing our present location. My illness has compelled us to a decision, which has for a long time been expected.

"You will be surprised to learn that we are to leave Norton, as soon as I am able to travel; and, if life be spared, shall hope to be with you, darling mother! once more, in a few weeks. Oh, my mother, it stops my breath to think of it! After so many years of separation, shall I indeed once more lay my head on your bosom—once more see the dear old home? But ah! what changes since last I stood beneath its shelter!

"It will be a sad return. After all, I have never half realized that *father* is no longer there. Whenever I think of 'Hill Farm,' my mind instinctively rests upon him, as the energetic and vigorous head. Being absent myself, his death has always seemed like a painful dream; and now, for the first time, it begins to feel like a sad reality.

"And I, too, have changed, my mother. Do not expect to see the rosy, healthy, merry daughter from whom you parted. Sickness, hard labor, and bereavements have followed one another very rapidly for the last few years, and have made me old before my time. You will hardly know me, mother.

"But I forget that all this time I am keeping you in ignorance of the causes which have made it advisable for us to leave our people here, and find a home elsewhere.

"As you will have suspected from our letters, since we came to Norton, our healths have suffered greatly from the effects of the climate. I do not think, however, that the climate should bear all the blame. It is no doubt very trying, and I do not believe there are many, in the easiest circumstances, that can remain here for any length of time, and not be affected in some degree by it. But added to this, we have been fitted for ready victims to the unhealthy influences by poor pay, and consequently over-work. It was hard enough when we lived in Glenville; but our church there was not culpable. They, most truly, did all they could, and the place was really a healthy one. Here, I regret to say, most of the blame must rest upon the negligence of a people who have ever, I doubt not, loved us truly, but could never realize that a devoted minister, such as my dear husband has been, was worthy of at least a comfortable support; and having given them his whole time, strength and thought, *such support* was only *justice*, not *charity*. But if their hearts have ever told them their duty, their practice has been entirely different. The sum they first pledged was only barely sufficient for our absolute necessities, used with strict economy, but with that we should have been well content—for we have never asked for luxuries—and are, and have ever been, willing to work hard, and live in the most primitive manner. But no one year have they ever paid us fully, and the little we have received has been by constant solicitation. Still we loved our people with an affection not easily chilled, and *because* we have thus loved them, we have submitted to the humiliation of buying that which *we must have* on credit, and securing the means to pay our own debts, by *dunning* our people for our just dues; or when our creditors would not receive the *promises*, that our demands obtained, as contentedly as if they were good gold, we have *tried hard* to meet their reasonable calls by the little I could gain by my needle, or by the increased labors of taking gentlemen to board, or the produce of our garden.

"This will seem a very strange, if not wholly improbable statement, to an eastern mind, and my mother will ask, 'Why did you not leave at once, when you found that they considered *fair promises* as a proper equivalent for their pastor's labors?'

"My only answer, dearest mother, must be, that we *loved* our church. We could not help it, little as you may think they deserved our interest; and besides, we felt, and still feel, sure that they reciprocated our affection. They are a very interesting and most lovable people, and in most things exceedingly generous; but they have never been trained to feel that a clergyman's promised salary was a business transaction, which they were as much bound in honor to pay as any other debt.

"Well, it is all over now. Our last year's salary is still partly unpaid, and much as they grieve at our leaving them, I doubt if even now they will make it up, or feel that their own short-comings have really been the main cause of severing the pleasant ties which have so long united us. But though we do not yet see how, the hardships we have passed through will not have been in vain. We feel that we shall have been, in some sense, pioneers, to prepare the way for other of our brethren to labor as successfully, and with less pecuniary hindrances; because the people will have learned that their spiritual teacher must have the means of comfortable living, if they would have his labors blessed with an abundant harvest.

"George has been solicited to come and take charge of the church, you used to know as Rev. Mr. Holdfast's. Twice he has declined, but the third application came when our affairs had reached a crisis that no longer admitted of temporizing or forbearance, and added to that, I was the same week taken ill. The physicians all agreed that I ought no longer to remain in this climate, or risk the probability of being obliged to exert myself so much beyond my strength, as heretofore. Brother Charles, greatly as he sorrows at the thought of a separation, is very decided as to our duty in this matter, and cousin Francis is just as eccentric in his manifestations of kindness and good will as ever.

"And now, dear mother, I must draw this long letter to a close. Soon, soon I shall be with you, I trust, and if God prospers us, shall be living near you. This is all very delightful. But there are other thoughts that are sad. I never imagined that the idea of a return to you, my mother, could be anything but unmixed joy. But here, if I have suffered much, I have enjoyed much. I love, very dearly, many here. Our labors and deprivations have brought George and myself together, as we never could have been, in a more prosperous, and comfortable settlement; and I dread, lest the larger field, and an entirely different class of duties for both, may naturally tend to separate us, or so divide our duties that we shall be less together.

I exceedingly shrink from associations which wil require a more formal etiquette, and will almost compel a less primitive style of living. I have a most inveterate dislike to city life and all its peculiarities, and would rather stay here and work till I die, than have George become like many city clergymen, whom I have had many opportunities of observing. And then there are some *little green graves* that I can never look upon again if I go away; but of these I may not speak, I am weak, yet, and it unnerves me. I will close now, and what else is to be told, my beloved mother must hear from the lips of her loving

"MARY."

And now, having followed our friends to the close of their western life, we will leave them for the present. A new path lies before—and whatever of care or trial may be hidden in it, for them, it will, most probably, be of a totally different nature. Some future day we may feel inclined to give our readers an opportunity to compare the past with the life upon which they enter as we bid them farewell.

We will offer no apologies for the minutenes of

detail which may have made this narrative tedious. A simple western home history was all that we promised, and abiding by the truth, we have made no attempt at sentiment, or display.

THE END.

THE

STANDARD FEMALE NOVELISTS.

THE WORKS OF JANE AUSTEN, Comprising "Pride and Prejudice," "Sense and Sensibility," "Mansfield Park," "Northanger Abbey," "Emma," and "Persuasion." First American edition. With steel vignettes. Complete in 4 vols., 12mo.

Price in Cloth, $4 00; *Sheep, library style,* $5 00; *Half calf, extra or antique,* $8 00.

THE WORKS OF HANNAH MORE, Comprising "Cœlebs in Search of a Wife," and her Tales and Allegories complete. With portrait on steel. 2 vols., 12mo.

Price, in Cloth, $2 00; *Sheep, library style,* $2 50; *Half calf, extra or antique,* $4 00.

THE WORKS OF JANE PORTER, Comprising "The Scottish Chiefs," and "Thaddeus of Warsaw." With steel portrait. 2 vols., 12mo.

Price in Cloth, $2 00; *Sheep, library style,* $2 50; *Half calf, extra or antique,* $4 00.

THE WORKS OF ANNE RADCLIFFE, Comprising "The Mysteries of Eudolpho," and "Romance of the Forest." With steel portrait. 2 vols., 12mo.

Price in Cloth, $2 00; *Sheep, library style,* $2 50; *Half calf, extra or antique,* $4 00.

THE WORKS OF CHARLOTTE BRONTE (Currer Bell), Comprising "Jane Eyre," "Shirley," and "Villette." Complete in 3 vols., 12mo.

Price in Cloth, $3 00; *Sheep, library style,* $3 75; *Half calf, extra or antique,* $6 00.

EVELINA; or, The History of a Young Lady's Introduction to the World. By Frances Burney (Mme. d'Arblay). With a Life of the Author by T. B. Macaulay. 12mo.

Price in Cloth, $1 00; *Sheep, library style,* $1 25; *Half calf, extra or antique,* $2 00.

CORINNE; or, Italy. By Madame de Stael. Translated by Isabel Hill, with Metrical Versions of the Odes by L. E. Landon. 12mo.

Price in Cloth, $1 00; *Sheep, library style,* $1 25; *Half calf, extra or antique,* $2 00.

*** The above will be sent by mail, post-paid, on receipt of price

W. H. Tinson, Printer and Stereotyper, 43 & 45 Centre St., N. Y.

W. H. Tinson, Printer and Stereotyper, 43 & 45 Centre St., N. Y.

W. H. Tinson, Printer and Stereotyper, 43 & 45 Centre St., N. Y.

THE WORKS OF ANNE RADCLIFFE.

Two vols., now ready.

Comprising "The Mysteries of Udolpho," and "Romance of the Forest." With steel portrait. 12mo.

Price in Cloth,	. . . .	$2 00
"	Sheep, library style, . .	2 50
"	Half calf, gilt or antique, .	4 00

Like the great painter with whom she has been compared, Mrs. Radcliffe loved to sport with the romantic and terrible—with the striking images of the mountain forests, the cloud and storm, wild banditti, ruined castles, half-discovered glimpses of visionary shadows of the invisible world which seem at times to cross our path, and which still haunt and thrill the imagination.

THE WORKS OF JANE PORTER.

Two vols., now ready.

Comprising "The Scottish Chiefs," and "Thaddeus of Warsaw." With steel portrait. 12mo.

Price in Cloth,	. . . .	$2 00
"	Sheep, library style, . .	2 50
"	Half calf, gilt or antique, .	4 00

"'Thaddeus of Warsaw,' 'which in our youth beguiled us of our tears,' is a favorite. It is to Miss Porter's fame that she began the system of historical novel-writing, which attained the climax of its renown in the hands of Sir Walter Scott. And no light praise it is that she has thus pioneered the way for the greatest exhibition of the greatest genius of our time. She may parody Bishop Hall, and tell Sir Walter:

'I first adventured—follow me who list,
And be *second* Scottish novelist.'"

Frazer's Magazine.

*** The above will be sent by mail, post-paid, on receipt of price.

W. H. TINSON, Printer and Stereotyper, 43 & 45 Centre St., N. Y.

LIBRARY OF SACRED CLASSICS.

PRINTED FROM NEW AND BEAUTIFUL LARGE (PICA) TYPE.

BUNYAN'S PILGRIM'S PROGRESS, 12mo., $1 00
THE SAME—full gilt sides and edges, ... 1 50
THE SAME—half calf antique, ... 2 00

DODDRIDGE'S RISE & PROGRESS, 12mo., 1 00
THE SAME—full gilt sides and edges, ... 1 50
THE SAME—half calf, antique, ... 2 00

BAXTER'S SAINTS' REST, 12mo., ... 1 00
THE SAME—full gilt sides and edges, ... 1 50
THE SAME—half calf, antique, ... 2 00

TAYLOR'S HOLY LIVING, 12mo., ... 1 00
THE SAME—full gilt sides and edges, ... 1 50
THE SAME—half calf, antique, ... 2 00

Other volumes of a similar character to follow.

John Bunyan! Philip Doddridge! Richard Baxter! Jeremy Taylor! "*Pilgrim's Progress,*" "*Rise and Progress,*" "*Saints' Rest,*" and "*Holy Living.*" What Authors! What Subjects! What Books! Writers for immortality on immortal subjects, familiar to every reader from early infancy—household names and words and books for our maturer years. They will live forever, and do good to all. Old and young alike can drink at this well, "pure and undefiled," certain of refreshing draughts of pure and wholesome literature.

*** The above will be sent by mail, post-paid, on receipt of price.

W. H. TINSON, Printer and Stereotyper, 43 & 45 Centre St., N. Y.

DERBY & JACKSON'S

STANDARD BRITISH CLASSICS.

IN FIFTEEN VOLUMES, COMPRISING:

BOSWELL'S JOHNSON,	Four Volumes.
ADDISON'S WORKS,	Six Volumes.
GOLDSMITH'S WORKS,	Four Volumes.
FIELDING'S WORKS,	Four Volumes.
SMOLLETT'S WORKS,	Six Volumes.
STERNE'S WORKS,	Two Volumes.
DEAN SWIFT'S WORKS,	Six Volumes.
JOHNSON'S WORKS,	Two Volumes.
DEFOE'S WORKS,	Two Volumes.
LAMB'S WORKS,	Five Volumes.
HAZLITT'S WORKS,	Five Volumes.
LEIGH HUNT'S WORKS,	Four Volumes.

Pronounced the most valuable and handsome set of books ever introduced into the American market. Put up in two elegant cases, bound in half calf antique, or half calf gilt. Price $2 25 per volume, or, per set, $112 50.

We also have the same works, bound in neat cloth, for $1 25 per volume; or sheep, library style for $1 50 per vol.

***** Either or all of the above will be sent by mail, post-paid, on receipt of price.**

W. H. Tinson, Printer and Stereotyper, 43 & 45 Centre St., N. Y.

THE

WORKS OF LEIGH HUNT,

Comprising his "Italian and English Poets," "Wit and Humor," "Essays," "Miscellanies," and "English Authors," 4 vols.

Price in Cloth,	$5 00
" Sheep, library style,	6 00
" Half calf, extra,	9 00
" Half calf, antique,	9 00

"We ought to say that nothing can be less formal than the style of Mr. Hunt's Essays. It reminds us of the manner of some of Steele's best papers. Indeed, since the death of Southey, we think Leigh Hunt the pleasantest writer we have. * * * An account was given in this Journal by an admirer of the only surviving member of a group of which Lamb was the central figure; it is probable that of this group Hazlitt was the man of highest intellectual powers—Lamb the person who sought to see everything in the point of view in which it could be most favorably seen—and Hunt, combining in a great measure both their powers, seems to have looked on life and books in a spirit of more thoughtful appreciation than either, and in a feeling more thoroughly genial."—*Dublin University Magazine.*

THE WORKS OF LORD CHESTERFIELD.

Comprising his "Letters to his Son." Complete in 1 *vol.*, 12*mo.*

Price in Cloth,	$1 25
" Sheep, library style,	1 50
" Half calf, extra,	2 25
" Half calf, antique,	2 25
" Full tree calf,	3 00

*** The above will be sent by mail, post-paid, on receipt of price.

W. H. Tinson, Printer and Stereotyper, 43 & 45 Centre St., N. Y.

www.ingramcontent.com/pod-product-compliance
Lightning Source LLC
LaVergne TN
LVHW010158110826
845151LV00002B/551